Rise & Fight

Charles E. Hayes

Charles E. Hayes

Small Batch Sour Mash Publishing LLC

318 Slate Lick St

London, Kentucky 40741

Copyright © 2017 Charles E. Hayes

All rights reserved.

ISBN: 1974340953
ISBN-13: 978-1974340958

DEDICATION

AMERICAN PATRIOTS
Especially the **AMERICAN VETERANS**

CONTENTS

	Acknowledgments	i
	Prologue	3
1	To South Carolina	11
2	Camp Talk	18
3	The Battle of Hobkirk's Hill	25
4	The Ambush	34
5	Camp Follower Gossip May 15, 1781	53
6	New Plans	66
7	Mission to Marion	75
8	Camp Follower Gossip July 11, 1781	86
9	Attack on Ninety-Six	102
10	Rising	112
11	The Battle of Eutaw Springs	127
12	Camp Follower Gossip October 25, 1781	150
	Epilogue	157
	About the Author	158
	Revolutionary War Pension Applications	160

ACKNOWLEDGMENTS

Historians, Authors, Artists, to a lot of people more capable than I that I have learned a great deal from with special thanks to US Air Force veteran and artist Robert W. Wilson for use of his work on the cover of this book

PROLOGUE

It was sometime in late March when we got back from spying on Cornwallis's army. We, me and Rob McLane, had stayed until we had a pretty good idea of which way Cornwallis was going to jump. I half expected him to return to Charlestown, South Carolina. In South Carolina, he could maybe get more men and supplies and work on defeating the militia left in South Carolina.

Of course, I half expected him to go north into Virginia. In Virginia, the traitor Benedict Arnold and General Phillips were raising quite a bit of ruckus and trying to mess up the system that was supposed to get supplies to General Greene's army in North Carolina.

I'd heard that General Greene figured that Cornwallis wouldn't go back to South Carolina. The figuring was that Cornwallis's army was so rundown and had lost so many men that he didn't want his fellow officers in Charlestown to realize how bad whipped his army really was.

From our spying, we were pretty certain that Cornwallis was taking his army north into Virginia.

We reported to some of General Greene's staff. They listened and wrote down some of what we told them. I kind of wanted to know which way we would jump next so I asked.

"Major, does this mean we are chasing Cornwallis into Virginia?"

"Could be but I don't think so."

"Aint the General worried that Cornwallis might turn back south and come in behind him while he's busy with some other army in front of him?"

"Not any more. Your friend, Sergeant Bowman, is in Virginia spying to make sure that doesn't happen."

"Dan?"

"Yes, Sergeant Daniel Bowman."

"I need to get up there with him."

"General Greene needs you with him here."

I didn't like it. I'd promised Dan's pa, my cousin, that I'd kindly watch him and guide him. I couldn't do that when I was in the Carolina's and he was in Virginia.

"What made you officers think he should be the one to go to Virginia?"

"You did. You were the one told us he was a sergeant."

That I had done. Dan had kept up with me when a lot of grown men couldn't. He could think fast and act fast. He didn't get rattled or excited. I had to say something but I was too choked to say anything.

"I guess I just hate to lose my spying partner."

"You still have McLane."

"Yes, I do." I didn't add to that. Rob McLane was a good lad. He'd been with me and Dan since right after the fight at Hannah's Cowpens. He had come a long way since he told his pa he was joining us and left with us. He had got better. After getting into too many fights, he had learned to think before he spoke. He no longer told Continental soldiers that the militia could do a better job than regular soldiers. He had been in battles, messed up by loading his musket and firing it without ever priming the pan until he had six charges in the barrel. It bothered him that, in his first battle, he hadn't lived up to what he expected of himself.

I reminded myself that he had got a lot better. He stopped a man who wanted to steal Dan's horse, Buford. He had managed to pull his weight. I almost wished I'd made him a sergeant and kept Dan though.

I knew deep down that Dan could do the job and handle himself just fine. Truth is, Rob still needed some looking after but he would be okay if I gave him a chance. It's just that Dan knew what I'd do before I did it and I pretty much knew him the same way.

I brought my thoughts back to where they should be and asked, "What will General Greene be wanting to get done now?"

"He'll be sending Colonel Lee and some of his legion down to around the Pee Dee and Santee Rivers to join up with General Marion. There was talk of sending you with him but Greene has other jobs for you to do."

As far as I'm concerned, we won at Guilford Courthouse. If the British won a victory at Guilford Courthouse, I hope they win five more just like it. I say the British didn't win at Guilford Courthouse. Of course, the British say and think they won a big victory at Guilford Courthouse. This just shows that the British aint got real good sense. Cornwallis not only lost a good part of his army, somewhere between a quarter and a third of it, but the British left the field without burying all of their dead. He left wounded on the battlefield to die because he didn't have enough men or wagons to carry them with him. Cornwallis had to leave the field for Wilmington because he didn't have enough supplies to stay put.

Greene left the battlefield with his soldiers marching and carrying a lot of their wounded. He took them to the place that was already prepared where they posted pickets and put out patrols, fed the army and kept right on soldiering. Greene's army didn't feel beaten. They felt like they had fought a good fight and were ready to fight another one.

Since the North Carolina militia had run the first time they got a chance, most of the regulars and quite a few of the other militia figured that they would have won the whole shebang if only the North Carolina militia had stood to fire their two or three volleys.

Sure, there was some disappointment because we hadn't whipped Cornwallis like we had whipped Tarleton at the Battle of the Cowpens. On the other hand, we hadn't been whipped like Gates had been whipped at Camden. As far as I was concerned - - - that made a big difference.

I heard that General Greene had said to his staff that Cornwallis might think he had won but, if so, it had ruined his army of redcoats because Cornwallis had to retreat to Wilmington. When I heard this, I figured that he was right because it was hard to declare a real victory when you had to retreat leaving wounded behind and your dead unburied.[1]

---

[1] *Sir Henry Clinton's comment on Cornwallis's victory at Guilford Court-house, ". . . from 3200 when he (Cornwallis) passed the Catawba in January he is reduced by sickness and desertion to 1300, and after the victory, which was brilliant, to 700. With those, without provisions or arms, he invites by*

Greene wanted first off to go after Cornwallis but he now had no mounted infantry because he had to send horses away because he couldn't feed them and the militias from North Carolina and Virginia wouldn't serve beyond the time they had signed up to serve on March 30, 1781.

Cornwallis escaped with his whipped victorious army to Wilmington, North Carolina. What Cornwallis didn't know was that the day after the battle of Guilford Courthouse, Captain Wade Hampton (I think he was still a captain) came to Greene with news of what was happening in South Carolina and fetched him a letter from General Sumter.

What Hampton and Sumter's letter said was that British posts between Charlestown and the west end of South Carolina could be picked easy as an apple on a low limb. That was when Green decided to send Light Horse Harry Lee and a bunch of his Legion to join up with General Marion to raise some cane with the British. When the army was supplied, rested and ready Greene headed us to South Carolina.

I don't know when Greene decided that his best move would be to join other American forces near Camden, South Carolina, but that is what he decided. Now General Greene could move an army quick when he had to but, right then, he didn't have to move quick. He made sure the wounded got tended to and supplies were ready and cached where he could have them when we needed them.

---

proclamation those poor people to join him .

It doesn't matter who or how many decided that it would be best for Greene to take his army into South Carolina and take on the British posts there, It doesn't matter because that is what we did and there aint no use crying about it now. Besides, we were following General Nathaniel Greene. We weren't following General Horatio Gates. If Greene hadn't himself won a big battle, he hadn't outrun his militia leaving the battlefield either.

The upshot of it was that Greene left Cornwallis to do whatever he decided to do and take the American army back to South Carolina. From what I gathered, the biggest part of Greene's army would go to the area around Camden leaving his two light corps to would join Marion and other Partisan groups.

The purpose was to mess up the supply lines between Charlestown and Camden and Ninety-Six, capture messages between British forces and generally make their lives miserable. Greene, having been General Washington's quartermaster general, knew that Camden and Ninety-six couldn't last without supplies and provisions from Charlestown.

Not everybody agreed with Greene's move. Some argued that the survival of the south depended on the safety and survival of Virginia. They figured that Greene should keep after Cornwallis. Greene seemed to figure that von Steuben and his help could hold Virginia while he wrecked the British plans in South Carolina.

Rob McLane, he was tickled to death to be in an army that hadn't been whipped. If he had a vote, he would have voted to stay in North Carolina close to his new wife. I thought he might decide to just stay but he didn't want to be that close to his new mother-in-law.

I don't reckon that it ever crossed Rob's mind to leave the army. He'd been with us since the Battle of the Cowpens and had got a right smart better than he was in January and February. So, I really wasn't surprised when he said that his new wife would be going with the army,

Contrary to what some folks think, most camp followers aint bawdy women. Wives and Children have followed the army to stay close to husbands and fathers. I guess there are hundreds, no, thousands of them.

Some nights, when my arms fest empty and I had things I needed to talk to somebody close about, I thought about sending for my wife. If I were a regular soldier and not militia - - - and if I were told that we were going to Pennsylvania or New York or somewhere far off, then I just might send for my wife. It's one thing to have to wait a few weeks or few months to be with my wife. I don't know as I could handle being away for a year or two.

Camp followers are both men and women. They helped by hauling supplies in their wagons, tending to the sick and wounded, cooking, washing laundry, and other such chores. Some of the women, but not most of them, were bawdy women and I guess they were needed by some men.

I know for a fact that at least two women marched beside their husbands disguised as soldiers and fought beside them. Other soldiers knew it to but they kept their silence. I wouldn't be surprised if some officers didn't know it.

I heard tale of a woman at the battle of Monmouth who was fetching water to her man's cannon crew when he got wounded (Or maybe he was killed - - - depends on who is telling the tale) and took his place firing the cannon. Soldiers say the woman, they called her Molly Pitcher and say her name was Polly Hayes - - - or maybe it was Mary Hayes - - - depends on who tells the tale.

Anyhow, a lot of good women followed the armies to be close to their men. I reckoned that Anna would follow Rob and be one of them.

Molly Pitcher at the Battle of Monmouth, by Alonzo Chapel Public Domain

1

To South Carolina

While General Greene moved his army south, Me and Rob went back to doing our spying for the army. There was still a lot of raiding and killing going on. There was still plenty of fighting and skirmishing going on and part of it was being done by the North Carolina militia.

I didn't have to see the fighting to know it was going on. Between Rob and Anna, I was told everything. I don't know which of them was the worse to gossip but there wasn't a rumor came within ten miles of the camp that they didn't hear it and tell me about it. Along with the rumors, they also picked up quite a bit of truth.

Rob's story

Right after Cornwallis left Ramsey's Mill and headed his army toward Wilmington, one of his foraging parties was attacked near Stuart's Ford. Captain John Taylor was patrolling with his dragoons when they saw part of the foraging party's guard detail. Taylor ordered attack and they attacked. They killed one or two and captured three.

Taylor received word from one of his spies that the British were coming so they waited for them. When the British, it was the Brigade of Guards, got in range, Taylor's men began shooting. The British seemed confused and it was beginning to look like a good victory when a British general took charge. I wasn't there but one of Taylor's men said that General O'Hara pushed the attack. The general was hurt and was carried on the back of a soldier from the 23rd Regiment Grenadiers across the creek. He was armed with a double barrel fusee that he shot at Taylor's men twice. Three of Taylor's men were wounded with buckshot. Taylor, being outnumbered, retreated before they could be surrounded and overwhelmed.

Seeing that the general had been wounded, I figure it was probably O'Hara because he was wounded at Guilford Courthouse

There was another scrape at Cole's Bridge. It seems that militia from Anson county North Carolina were moving supplies from Cross Creek to Haley's Ferry in a hurry. They were moving fast trying to keep the British from finding out about the supplies and trying to take them.

They were moving as fast as they could but they still got attacked. They were attacked near Cole's Bridge on Drowning Creek by the British. I was told that they were attacked by nearly 500 men, Tory militia and British soldiers. The Patriot militia had to run because they were outnumbered by 5 to 1. The militia from Anson County were routed.by the redcoats.

The British captured seven of the militia and killed or wounded a handful. The British took all the supplies, wagons, horses and slaves. Less than two dozen militia were left together when the battle was over. Over twice that number were running toward Anson County.

Anna's story

The other women told me that the British lost four killed and about that many wounded. Greene lost some supplies that we sure couldn't afford to lose. Some corn meal that was already loaded on boats at Haley's Ferry.

I reckon that the worse action was the massacre at Rouse House. The British commander at Wilmington Major Craig sent out a bunch of men to bring in cattle from some of the farms. These cattle were bad needed to feed Cornwallis's army which was on its way there. The advance guard of the cattle thieves were told that a bunch of Patriots drinking ale at Alexander Rouse's Tavern, about eight miles north of Wilmington.

The Patriots a drinkin in the tavern were light cavalry sent out spying by General John Alexander Lillington to find and drive off cattle before the British could steal them. I guess the cavalry men figured they needed a planning meeting at Rouse's Tavern before they got down to the business of following orders.

The British were also told that two of the men at the tavern were Major Jim Love and Private William Jones of the New Hanover County Militia. Both were known to and wanted by the British in Wilmington. The two men would ride into Wilmington, shoot British sentinels, wait for the dragoons to chase them, and lead the dragoons into an ambush.

Major Craig, commander at Wilmington, was sure a man of habit. It became his habit to ride out on the Newberne road every evening after he ate his supper. He would have with him Captain Gordon and twelve to fifteen dragoons. Major Love saw that this habit of Major Craig's and decided to ambush him. He got over 25 men and lay in ambush in a thick swamp around mile outside of Wilmington. Love knew that the British rode across bridges in single file.

Major James Love told his men to pick off the British when they were crossing a bridge. When the militia, they weren't the best militia, heard the dragoons coming toward them and saw the red coats, one of them ran and most of the others followed. This left Major Love and Private Jones to face between twelve and twenty British, to face them all by themselves.

Major Love, he pointed his musket at Major Craig, aimed and took a deep breath. He let out half a breath and was ready to shoot when Private Jones talked him into leaving. Jones told him that one shot from them would be suicide because the dragoons would then charge them and kill them. Love and Jones left without either shooting his weapon.

The British were sure eager for the chance to bag Major Love. Major Craig sent out soldiers from the 82nd regiment to attack the American militia at Rouse's Tavern with orders to take no prisoners and to give no quarter. They rode to Rouse's Tavern to follow orders.

At Rouse's Tavern, the American militia men were celebrating. They were trying to drown the sorrow of losing, farms, friends and the peace they had known. They had been in danger of being attacked so long that they were used to the threat. Drinking, toasting friends who had fallen in battle, and generally trying to place distance between themselves and the war; The militia lost track of time until they realized it was almost midnight. Seeing that it was late and they were well in their cups, they went to sleep on the tavern floor.

Major Love was woke up by the sounds of almost a hundred redcoats surrounding the tavern. He woke the sleeping militia and grabbed his saddle. He could hear the British using crowbars to pry the tavern door open.

"Men, I'm not dying in here!"

Deciding to make the British pay for his life, he held the saddle in front of himself and kicked open the tavern door. Using his saddle to shield himself, he slashed with his long knife, slashing his way out of the tavern. He slashed and stabbed his way for about a hundred feet before he fell, killed by the stabs of British bayonets.

The attacking British didn't deliberately spare any militiaman in the tavern. A few made it out but the rest were killed even those who tried to surrender. Around a dozen militia were killed inside the tavern. One man was promised freedom if he told the redcoats where other militia were hiding. Surrounded by his dead and dying comrades, the man told where others were hiding. After he talked, the redcoats murdered him too.[2]

While the massacre was going on, Colonel Bloodworth heard the gunfire at the tavern and he got a bunch of his militia to go see what was going on. They got to the tavern to find the British gone and Major Love outside the tavern stabbed to death. They went into the tavern to find the tavern floor covered with dead militia and covered with blood and gore. They found out that the redcoats refused to give quarter from an old woman who sat near the fireplace with three or four young children.

She also told Bloodworth that some British had been wounded. Bloodworth and his men checked and found the blood trails left by wounded redcoats.

"Men, I'm going to revenge this!"

Rob's story of the battle at Wolf's Den

The fighting in North Carolina continued. We were already in South Carolina by the time the battle at Wolf's Den was fought. Colonel Cleveland had returned to his farm on the south fork of the New River. The Tory, Captain Will Riddle, was told that Colonel Cleveland had returned to his farm. Riddle went after Cleveland.

Riddle had some of his Troy militia steal Colonel Cleveland's horse. They tied the horse where it could be seen and set up an ambush for Cleveland. It was a good plan because Cleveland and

---

[2] See Revolutionary Pension Applications at the end of the book for further information.

a man named Richard Calloway went looking for the horse. When they found the horse, Riddle and his Tories began shooting at them. Cleveland carried two pistols and Calloway was unarmed except for a belt knife.

Calloway was shot in the leg and Cleveland grabbed a Tory woman unfortunate enough to be there and shielded Calloway with her. He got Riddle to agree to ransom Cleveland and Calloway and not kill them.

Neither Cleveland nor Callaway trusted Riddle to keep his word but they figured to buy some time to figure out how to escape.

Cleveland and Calloway were taken to Wolf's Den. They broke overhanging limbs to mark their trail. They arrived at the cave on Riddle's knob called Wolf's Den. This was the hideaway of Captain Riddle and his Tory militia.

Joe Calloway learned real quick that the two were captured and went to see Rob Cleveland, the colonel's younger brother. Hearing what had happened, Rob rounded up a bunch of the colonel's men and they took off to find the colonel.

The next morning, the Tories at Wolf's Den fixed breakfast but kept Colonel Cleveland well guarded. One of the Tories held one of the colonel's pistols to his head. Captain Riddle told Cleveland to write passes saying that each of the Tories was a good Patriot.

Cleveland was certain that as soon as the passes were written that he would be killed. Looking around, trying to find a way to escape, Cleveland apologized for his slowness. He added that he was trying to write neatly.

Cleveland was still writing the passes when his brother and the Patriot militia arrived and attacked. Cleveland had been sitting on a downed tree trunk while he wrote the passes. He rolled off and used the downed tree trunk as shelter from the musket fire. Riddle escaped with only one Tory wounded. Three days later, Riddle and his men were caught. They were court martialed and Riddle, Reeves, and Goss were found guilty and hanged.

"Colonel Cleveland, he was the head officer at the court martial. Now you tell me Nate, why are we in South Carolina with so much going on in North Carolina?"

"Rob, it's like this, General Greene wasn't leaving North Carolina because there was no fighting. He left North Carolina to roll back British gains in South Carolina. All the piddling militia skirmishes in North Carolina will go on as long as the war lasts. Greene figures that by pushing back British gains in South Carolina, he'll be doing more to end and win the war."

2

Camp Talk

Greene ordered Kirkwood to take and hold Logtown if it were possible. Kirkwood captured eleven British soldiers as prisoners. He attacked Logtown and after arriving there about 9 at night. He had captured the town by midnight. The British kept up a scattered fire all night. The British attacked at daybreak and there was a short but sharp battle. The battle ended with the British retreating. Kirkwood's force was on edge waiting for a larger British force to attack when they saw Greene's army approaching.

Logtown was burning, houses were afire and the houses were falling down in flames. Rawdon ordered everything destroyed before we could use the shelter and materials for our benefit. When the outer patrols returned to Camden, they had tried to burn Logtown. General Greene kept his army there for three days, in full view of the British at Camden.

Our riflemen would get close enough the British lines and shoot at the sentries and British soldiers who came within range. It's hard to say whether the British started the shooting or the Americans started shooting first. Maybe both sides got the idea about the same time.

Camden is located on a peninsula formed by Pine Tree Creek

on the east, and the Wateree on the west. Six forts the forts stretching across an area cleared of all trees and brush for almost a mile on each side. The six forts were called by the numbers 1 through 6. The fort closest to Pinetree Creek being number 1 and number 6 closest to the Wateree in the west. The British hospital and the ferry were both covered by a fort .

The second day at Logtown, Colonel Webb's battalion of militia insisted that their time was up and demanded to be relieved to return home to North Carolina. No one believed them, I sure didn't. I figured they were just too womanish to risk a fight with the British. Greene refused and one of their captains, I believe it was Captain Noballs, said the North Carolina would mutiny of he didn't take them home. I guess he would have to tuck them in too. They could not be talked into staying and acting like men. The men in that militia were in a hurry to leave danger and run home. General Greene was disgusted but he directed Colonel Williams to write their discharges. Greene ordered Colonel Webb to take them back to North Carolina.

General Greene kept us camped there and sent out patrols. Before dark, our light troops would be swapping shots with some of the British patrols. Some of our men recognized the uniforms of the New York Volunteers, and the Volunteers of Ireland on the men they were fighting.

Greene sent Washington's dragoons and Kirkwood's infantry to spy the defenses around Camden. They circled Camden. They burned a house in one of the British defense positions on the Wateree River, liberated forty horses and over fifty head of cattle.

Camden was the most important British post outside of Charlestown. After Cornwallis seized Camden in 1780, the British built four small defensive forts at the four corners of Camden and a fifth north of town on the Salisbury Road. A large stockade, surrounded by high walls, was in the middle of town. Greene stayed long enough to decide that Camden's defenses were too strong for him to take with the forces he had with him.

I was getting more impressed at how fast Rob was learning. It wasn't that long ago that he's spout off his opinion about anything even if he didn't have an opinion. That carelessness caused him more than one fight - - - like the time he explained to soldiers from the Maryland Line that militia were much better fighters than regular army soldiers. Now, he looks to others to find out what they think about something and add that to what he knows. On the early evening of April 24^{th,} he brought two militiamen to seek my opinion.

"Nate, we was arguing about why Cornwallis run off to Wilmington. Was he scared of Greene or what? And why did Greene bring us to South Carolina? Was he afraid of Cornwallis?"

I studied the questions a bit before I gave an answer.

"The truth is, I didn't see Cornwallis taking his army from the Carolinas to Virginia as a good move when he did it and I don't see the sense of it now. The only thing I have ever been able to come up with is that Cornwallis was whipped and knew it. Still, I figured it was reckless to leave the British army in the Carolina's with only the British navy and local Tory militias for support. The British navy was already busy and the Tory militias could be depended on about as much as some of the Patriot militia could be depended on. The French can still attack."

"There's no French here."

:"French fleets could show up any time on the Atlantic coasts the southern colonies – I mean southern states. The French could show up any time with transports full of French soldiers. The many Tory militias could change sides any time it was to their best interest. We have word that Cornwallis is going to Virginia. By going to Virginia with his army, Cornwallis will expose British forces in South

Carolina and Georgia to attacks by the Continental army and Partisan forces."

"Can we whip them?"

"I figure that without Cornwallis and his attack dog, Tarleton, our job will be easier. The only trouble was, I want to tangle with Tarleton again. I'm not the only one. Both Colonel Washington and Colonel Lee want to prove that they are better than Tarleton."

Rob pointed to one of the militiamen with him, "Nate, he thinks that Greene left North Carolina because he's afraid of Cornwallis. Do you think Greene's afraid of Cornwallis?"

"Our army, led by General Nathanael Greene has stayed alive despite all the British army has done trying to destroy us. Cornwallis destroyed Gates at Camden but General Greene aint Gates. While Cornwallis is heading to Virginia, Greene brought us to South Carolina to cripple the British here. Greene wants to place us in a spot where we can destroy all the British posts and garrisons by attacking with a bigger force than they can handle. Greene will take us to attack the British garrisons in the back country of South Carolina and Georgia. He's already sent for General Francis Marion and other patriot forces to join us here.

"Just where is here?"

"Hobkirk's Hill.".

"Do you think General Greene can handle the British? Do the British think Greene is a good general?"

"If the British didn't figure out by the end of the Battle of Guilford Courthouse that Green is a good general, then they aint paying attention. He led his army over three hundred miles to cross the Dan River into Virginia. Three hundred miles with Cornwallis doing his best to pin the

American army against a river and destroy it. He chose the battlefield and fought Cornwallis at Guilford Courthouse. True, Cornwallis stayed on the field and Greene's army drew back to a defensive camp with dry shelter, food and medical help for our wounded."

"But Cornwallis won, didn't he?"

"Cornwallis had held the field but his redcoat army lost too many men. He quit chasing after Greene and hightailed it to Wilmington North Carolina on the coast. Wilmington was a good two hundred miles from Guilford Courthouse. Greene followed Cornwallis to Cross Creek until we ran low on food and some militia began to leave and go home. The Virginia militia left because their term was up."

One of the militiamen interrupted, "I guess that don't say much for the Virginia militia, does it?

"The Virginia militia held at Guilford Courthouse. When they got pushed back, they fought while they were pushed back. They bought the Continentals time and killed a sight of redcoats. There term was up and they went home. Their reason going home was more real than what the North Carolina militia used a few days ago."

"Oh."

"We – and I mean the soldiers in Greene's army – know that General Greene is a fighting man. He's able to attack. We know it would take a much bigger force to slow us down – let alone stop us."

"Rob said our spies found out that Cornwallis is going into Virginia. Why?"

"Why Cornwallis left the Carolina's while General Greene still had his army here is a question that I can't answer. Our spying found that Cornwallis was ordered to stay In the Carolinas and protect Charleston and the other posts and garrisons in South Carolina even if it meant he had to stop some of his attacks. Clinton's aim was that Cornwallis was only to move north when there was no threat to any of the posts or garrisons. I have no idea how Clinton will feel when he hears Cornwallis has moved his army north to Virginia."

"Can Greene beat the British in South Carolina?"

"General Greene is a doing man. Not like some men who get rattled and decide to do something even if it's wrong but a man who thinks before he acts. We chased after Cornwallis's army for over 60 miles. We had captured British soldiers and over 70 wounded British soldiers who Cornwallis had left behind at Guilford Courthouse. Greene had to give up the chase when our provisions and supplies got too low and the Virginia militia went home. Greene can handle the British in South Carolina."

"What did Cornwallis do when Greene stopped following him?"

"While Greene moved to South Carolina, Cornwallis kept right on retreating to Wilmington. He stopped for a spell at Cross Creek to tell the countryside that he had whipped Greene and try to enlist a bunch of militia. A lot of Tories came to the British camp and looked at the British army. They saw that Cornwallis's army was plumb wore out with a lot less men than they had expected. The Tories told Cornwallis that he was doing a good job and they would study about joining his army. They might have studied on joining but they didn't join. We heard that they rode into the camp, shook hands and said they were sure glad to see the British army, shook hands again and then rode home. The word I got was that none joined the British army. Cornwallis kept right on telling anybody who would listen that his campaign was a big success. His army had over 4,000 men after Charlestown fell. Less than a year later, his army has less than 2,000 soldiers. Greene didn't brag none but, before the British could send more men to South Carolina, he invaded South Carolina."

"Will Greene get a lot of help?"

"Except for South Carolina militia led by the likes of Marion and Sumter, we are on our own. The British will be keeping Lafayette and von Steuben too busy in Virginia for them to send us any help. "

"There's a lot of British in South Carolina. How will we handle them?"

"Those poor British. They only outnumber us by about four to one. They don't have enough of an advantage. Their army is scattered over a bunch of posts that have to be supplied and provisioned while they protected towns, river crossings, and military stores from attacks by the partisan bands led by The Swamp Fox (General Francis Marion), The Gamecock (General Thomas Sumter) and smaller bands of militias who wanted to avenge wrongs done by the British and Tory militias."

"Why are we here now, on Hobkirk's Hill?"

"Greene figured that the best place to start would be attacking Camden. Lord Rawdon is in command of about 1,000 experienced British soldiers there. Greene brought us across deep rivers, swamps and flooded creeks to Camden. Me, Rob McLane and other spies got there ahead of Greene. We didn't like what we saw. Even Rob, who figures we could whip anything, wondered."

Rob asked me, "Nate what do you think?"

I asked him, "What do you see Rob?"

Rob told me "It's pretty strong. I don't think we have enough cannon to take the earthworks. I don't think we have enough men or cannon to take it by siege. Of course, Washington dragoons and Kirkwood's infantry rode around Camden and spied it out. They also agreed that Camden was too well defended to take with the number of men and cannons that we have.

I was surprised at how much Rob had learned. I felt a little proud too. So, I told him "You might be right, Rob, you might be right."

We had reported to General Greene. He then sent out Colonel Washington's patrol to check what we reported and after Washington's report decided not to attack yet. Then we set up this defensive camp a few miles from Camden here at this wooded ridge folks hereabouts call Hobkirk's Hill. It looks like we'll have a standoff for a spell. We don't have enough men to attack Camden and Rawdon don't know how weak we are and likely he won't attack us.

That's the way it would have been, too. It would have been except that a deserter told the British that that our army had a weak defense spread over a wide circle with too little arms and ammunition. He also reported that Lee's Legion had been sent to find General Marion and wasn't with Greene. He told the British that while Greene had around 1,400 soldiers counting militia, he had just over 800 fit for duty.

3

The Battle of Hobkirk's Hill

Rawdon decided that with just shy of a thousand men and surprise, he could beat Greene. Rawdon attacked us less than a day after I said he wouldn't, on April 25th.

What I didn't know when I predicted that neither side would attack was that that day, April 24, Rawdon listened to a deserter, a Maryland drummer, who had fought only hours earlier alongside his brothers in a raid near Camden. He told Rawdon Greene's order of battle. He also told that Thomas Sumter and Francis Marion, leaders of bands of militia raising dickens with the British in South Carolina, would soon be joining Greene's army.

To make it worse, Rawdon heard of the fall of Fort Watson, a key link in the British supply chain across South Carolina. The loss of the outpost and Sumter's and Marion's militias running wild and ambushing his supply trains would cut Camden off from the main British force at Charlestown. Rawdon knew he had to act now before his army was out of food. He knew that if Camden fell, many of the other posts would have to surrender, face defeat or fall back to Charlestown.

Rawdon knew that Greene had about men than he did but he gambled that a bold attack would surprise Greene. Her also gambled that the militia wouldn't help Greene much. Rawdon armed musicians, drummers, everyone that could carry a musket and marched to attack Greene.

Rawdon followed the example set by Cornwallis at Camden and Tarleton on his raids, he attacked. Thanks to the deserter. Rawdon knew that Colonel Carrington had left for Rugeley's Mill. Rawdon decided to attack Greene before he got help from Carrington or Marion. Knowing that Greene had no cannon made the idea seem real good.

The morning after I told Rob and his friends that we had a standoff because Rawdon didn't know how weak we were, Rawdon attacked. He marched his army out of Camden at nine o'clock in the morning of the 25th of April Rawdon didn't come the most direct way where we could see him easy, he kept close to the edge of the swamp of Pine Tree Creek, hidden by the woods. He got his army ready to attack on the left of the American line. He used the same order of battle that Cornwallis had used against Gates the summer before. His first line was the Volunteers of Ireland. He put the New York Volunteers in the center, and the King's American Regiment on the left. His reserve was the South Carolina Provincial Regiment and the New York Dragoons

Rawdon took us by surprise. None of us were ready or expecting to be attacked. I sure didn't expect to be attacked. A lot of officers, were washing their feet. Many of the soldiers were washing kettles. Some were cleaning weapons and equipment. Men were passing out provisions and washing clothing. Many were just resting thinking there was no danger.

We found out different when the pickets were driven back. Greene and his staff were just finishing their meal when the attack began.

Greene's line of battle was the two Virginia regiments, under General Isaac Huger placed on the right of the road, the Fourth led by Colonel Campbell, and the Fifth led by Colonel Hawes. The two Maryland regiments, led by Colonel Otho H. Williams, held the left, with the First Maryland under Colonel Gunby, and the Fifth under Colonel Ford. The reserve was Colonel Washington's cavalry and the North Carolina militia under Colonel Read. Greene's few cannon were hidden behind the Fifth Virginia and the First Maryland. Patrols were sent out to spy on the country but we were sent north of Camden. On Greene's right, two strong pickets, commanded by Captain Morgan and Captain Benson and supported by Captain Kirkwood of Delaware, with what was left of his brave and experienced command.

The army didn't know that the British were coming until the pickets spotted them and shot at the redcoats. The pickets then fell back, shooting as they retreated. When the British got close to Greene's lines, the cannon were brought out and grapeshot was rained on the British.

Greene's center of Continental infantry marched right up to meet the British at the bottom of Hobkirk's Hill. It looked to me like we had the British right where we wanted them. I figured that when it came to fighting close, that the British wouldn't have a chance.

General Greene thought that he had the battle pretty much the way he wanted it and victory would be ours. He wasn't the only one who thought so. Most of us figured that all we had to do was hit the British flanks and we would hem them in and have our victory. Hawes's Virginians, Gunby's Marylanders, Campbell's Virginians on the right, and Ford's Marylanders on the left were in position to attack the British flanks. Greene ordered a counter attack. He ordered Washington to attack the

British rear and the units on the flanks to attack.

But Rawdon was commanding well drilled soldiers and he reacted to Greene's attack quickly. It helped that he knew what Greene's line of battle would be. Rawdon called his support and spread his line to expose the American right wing. When our soldiers tried to attack the British flanks, Rawdon's support outflanked them. The surprise of the attack by Rawdon's support drove back Greene's flanking wings and confused our center.

Our left wing held and had a chance to win the day against the best soldiers that Rawdon had in his command. It was the First Maryland against the Sixty-third Regiment of the line, and the King's American Regiment. The problems started when contradictory orders were given. Before it could be corrected, Captain Beatty, the First Maryland's leader, was shot in the heart and was killed. Those closest to Beatty stopped. Before order could be restored, Greene's attack was stopped. The officers tried to rally the soldiers but Colonel Ford was killed and the First Maryland first faltered, then retreated.

The retreat of the First Maryland, heroes of the Battle of the Cowpens and Guilford Courthouse, surprised Greene and his army. Greene was riding to rally the flank attack when he saw that his center was halted. He sped his horse to the center so that he could see the battle and discovered that his army was falling back on all sides.

Only Hawes' regiment was still together. Greene's cannons were abandoned. I've got to give Greene credit for his leadership. He was on top of a rise. He was easy to see and recognize. I think half Rawdon's .men were shooting at him. Despite the danger, he gave orders as calmly as if he were playing cards, He ordered Captain Smith, commanding a light infantry company from the Maryland line to save the cannon. As the British charged toward the cannon, shouting and sure they would capture the cannons, Greene jumped from his horse and grabbed the cannons' ropes. Captain Smith's men, seeing what General Greene was doing, rushed to the cannon and pulled the cannon toward safety. The British fought hard to capture the cannon. Captain Smith started the fight with forty-five men and was now down to fourteen. The British were close to capturing the guns when Colonel Washington and his dragoons charged the British and saved the cannon.

To be honest, I'm surprised that General Greene got out of that fight without a scratch. He rallied enough men to fight a rear-guard action and protect both our cannon and our retreat. No sir, Greene isn't just a doing man - - - General Greene is a fighting man!

I've got to say this, Rob McLane fought well. Just over two months earlier, he couldn't fire his musket because he had rammed his paper cartridge down the muzzle lead ball first. He then loaded it several times and didn't know the musket wasn't firing. Today. He loaded and fired like a trained soldier. He didn't notice when the army started to retreat until I grabbed his arm and pulled him back.

His cannon safe, Greene ordered that the wounded be carried away and ordered the retreat. It was a good steady military retreat, not a rout. While Rawdon stayed on the battlefield, Greene held his army together for almost three miles before stopping. He sent a detail to gather up stragglers and help the injured reach the American army. He rested his army there and took care of the wounded until late afternoon. Afterwards, he took his army to Sanders's Creek where his army camped.

Some say that if the Battalion of the Maryland Line had at least rallied, that we would have whipped Rawdon that day. They may be right but I got nothing ill to say about the Maryland Line. Their actions at the Battle of the Cowpens won the battle for General Morgan and they did a good job at Guilford Courthouse too.

The British would claim victory but then they claimed

victory every time one of them sneezed. What they don't realize is that just because we retreat - - - we aint whipped. Yes, the British stayed on the battlefield and claimed victory, but our army was still whole and we were still camped close to Camden after the battle. Like Cornwallis at Guilford Courthouse, Rawdon lost a fourth of his men killed, wounded or captured.

I could see that General Greene was real sad and down after we didn't whip Rawdon. He had been in lost battles before at Brandywine, Germantown and of course, Guilford Courthouse. Hobkirk's Hill hurt more than the others because he was afraid it meant that his plan to invade South Carolina was over. He was real put out that Sumter hadn't joined him when he sent for him. He figured that if the South Carolina militia had joined him that Rawdon wouldn't have had a chance.

Camp gossip from Anna (who got it from the woman who washed General Greene's clothing) had it that Greene said, "We fight, get beat, rise, and fight again."

Thinking on it, I don't think we recovered from the surprise of Rawdon's approach. I've noticed that surprise can be a big advantage and that day, the British surprised us. It also came to my mind that If Greene had just one more general, things would have been different. Things would have been different if General Daniel Morgan had been with us. Lucky for the British, General Morgan was in Virginia recovering from a bad attack of rheumatism.

I heard that Greene also began second guessing his sending Colonel Lee and his legion to hook up with General Francis Marion. Lee's Legion could have made a real big difference at Hobkirk's Hill.

All of Greene's second guessing his decisions stopped when he got word from Light Horse Harry.

Colonel Henry ("Light Horse Harry") Lee's legion of dragoons and light infantry had found the Swamp Fox, General Francis Marion. Lee and Marion joined forces and right off, they captured Fort Watson.

Lee and Marion set out to capture the walled British forts guarding supply lines between Charlestown and Camden. Fort Watson was their first target. From what I heard, they did a real fine job.

Fort Watson was built on top of an Indian mound and the stockade was by three rings of sharpened logs and poles pointing outward. The fort could have easily been taken with canon but neither the Swamp Fox Fort Watson's garrison showed that they could and would fight.

Lee and Marion weren't making any progress at taking the fort when a Major with the South Carolina militia came up with an idea. Major Hezekiah Maham said that his men could build a tower that would let our riflemen fire into the fort. He explained that the tower would be built of crossed timbers and be built higher than the stockade walls. He said that protected platforms would let our riflemen fire through loop holes and down into the garrison.

Not everyone was convinced but he was told to go ahead and he did. His men cut the poles and notched them in the cover of the forest. They assembled the tower at night and our riflemen began shooting British soldiers who thought themselves safe inside the garrison.

Soldiers inside the garrison soon realized that any movement made them a target of the riflemen in the tower, which was now called the Maham Tower. The fort with 120 British soldiers, surrendered.

(The capture of Fort Watson was the beginning of the end of the chain of British posts and forts in South Carolina. Within a month, Lee and Marion had besieged and captured Fort Motte. We heard that to capture fort Motte, they used fire arrows. Fort Motte and 184 British soldiers was captured.)

    I heard that Greene figured that the loss of forts that were to protect the moving of supplies and Greene's army watching the area would force Rawdon to abandon Camden. He was sure Camden didn't have more than two or three weeks of supplies on hand.

    Despite what happened on Hobkirk's Hill, I still have a high opinion of both General Greene and the Maryland Line. Like I said, I think that the surprise attack took us a while to get over. It's one thing to be ready for an attack and another to be relaxing and thinking there would be no attack. I figured the answer was for us to do the surprising.

4

Ambush

Rob and me didn't get much rest. Late on the day of the battle, Colonel Rawdon returned to Camden to tend to his wounded men. He didn't wait long but left right after the Battle of Hobkirk's Hill. He didn't take all of his men with him though. He left Captain Coffin at the battlefield because according to the custom they fought under, it was only a win if some of your force stayed on the battlefield. I don't understand why but the British felt that a part of his force had to stay on the battlefield to show that the British won the battle. I don't understand that thinking but then I aint a British colonel.

We were out early the next morning. The whole army wasn't out early the next morning, just me and Rob and a few other spies. Out patrol led us to Hobkirk's hill where we saw Captain Coffin's patrol. We were on our way back when we met up with Colonel Washington.

One of the first things that General Green did the morning after the battle was to send Colonel Will Washington and some of his dragoons to patrol and to spy the area. Well, like I said, we met up with Washington and told him that we had seen Coffin and his mounted infantry loafing on the Battlefield. I didn't think I had to say more and I didn't. Colonel Washington saw right off that he could trick the British into an ambush.

Washington hid most of his men in the woods and brush beside the Waxhaw road. When they were set, he sent me along with a hand full of men to get Coffin's attention. I knew I had to go along because I knew right where Coffin and his patrol were at. When Coffin and his men saw me and the rest of the men from Washington's patrol, they jumped up ready to fight. Like we planned, we acted scared and confused and lit out like we were trying to get away. The British were just tickled to death to have some scared Continentals and militia to beat up on so they were after us in a hurry. We stayed just far enough ahead of them and rode first to the Waxhaw road then down the Waxhaw road. We acted like we were kicking and beating our horses, trying to get them to run faster, but we weren't. We didn't want the patrol to get too far behind us and give up the chase.

We did a good job of convincing the British that we were running scared because they didn't think anything was wrong until Colonel Washington and the rest of his patrol ambushed them. Their shooting was real good because they killed or wounded over half of Coffin's Patrol. After the ambush, Captain Coffin's patrol - - - at least what was left of it - - - got back to Camden and Colonel Rawdon just as fast as they could.

We kept on patrolling. Part of our patrol was capturing any British messenger that we might come across. A lot of times, we didn't see any messengers. We didn't on that day but several days later, we did.

We saw the messenger with two other British soldiers riding in the direction of Charlestown. We knew where we could get to a creek crossing ahead of them so we rode straight across the country to get there first. We had time to water our horses and get them out of sight before the British got there.

When the British got out of their saddles to water their horses and stretch, I still wasn't sure how we could catch the three of them but I decided a little lying wouldn't hurt.

I hollered out, "British patrol, we're the Swamp Foxes men! Move away from your horses and guns or we'll kill you all right here!"

One of the men started toward his horse and Rob shot him in his upper leg. The other two looked like they had a notion but they didn't move.

"That man got off lucky! You two stay away from the horses and tie a bandage around his leg! Don't make any moves that might scare us and tie that bandage real tight!"

The two British soldiers did exactly like they were told but they began to whisper and I thought they might be getting brave so I hollered again.

"You men, shut up. Nate, you and Rob go up there and make sure they behave! We'll shoot them if they move wrong!

Rob and me, we moved up on them from different directions. I nudged one of the soldiers with my musket barrel and got his attention.

"You! Go take the bridle off the near horse and loop a rope around its neck!"

This is the kind of situation that made me miss Dan Bowman more than usual. Rob was a lot better than he was when he joined up with us but he couldn't read my mind yet and sometimes I thought Dan could.

"Now! Put the wounded man in the saddle! Tie him to it!"

He tied the wounded man to the saddle and waited to be told what to do next.

"Tie the neck rope to that tree! Then get on the horse behind him and sit still."

He did as he was told. I turned to the last British soldier and tossed him some rope. He caught the rope and I could see that he was looking for a way out.

"Tie your friend to the horse and get on behind him!"

"That horse can't carry three of us!"

"If I shoot you dead, it won't have to! Do as you're told to do!"

"Rob, start with their legs and tie them all together. If they make any trouble, we'll shoot them to pieces."

They didn't make trouble and I checked their pouches for messages. I found one from Colonel Rawdon to General Cornwallis. It read:

"After the action of the 25th of April, (an account of which I had the honour of transmitting to your lordship) Major General Greene remained for some days behind the farthest branch of Granny's Quarter Creek. A second attempt upon his army could not, in that situation, be undertaken upon the principle which advised the former. In the first instance, I made so short an excursion from my works, that I could venture, without hazard, to leave them very slightly guarded; and I had the confidence, that, had fortune proved unfavorable, we should easily have made good our retreat, and our loss, in all probability, would not have disabled us from the farther defense of the place. To get at General Greene in his retired situation, I must have made a very extensive circuit, in order to head the creek, which would have presented to him the fairest opportunity of slipping by me to Camden; and he was still so superior to me in numbers, that, had I left such a garrison at my post as might enable it to stand an assault, my force in the field would have been totally unequal to cope with the enemy's army. I had much to hope from the arrival of reinforcements to me, and little to fear from any probable addition to my antagonist's force."

We tied the weapons and pouches to the other two horses and

began out ride back to General Greene. We hadn't more than got started when someone called out to us.

"If you all with Marion, we want to surrender too."

Talk about being caught by surprise! I'd no idea that anyone else was near. The first thing I wanted to do was get out of there and to somewhere else - - - anywhere else - - - just as quick as I could but I didn't. I tried to act like I was backed up by General Marion, General Washington and the whole Continental Army.

That is not a problem. Ride out of the brush with your muskets held by the butts, muzzle down! Quick now!"

Slowly, five men rode out of the brush holding their muskets just like I told them to do. They didn't look any different from hundreds of other militiamen in South Carolina. No different except that they all had the look of someone who had seen something that they wanted to forget. That's the way I sized them up anyway.

"Real slow now, back man first, shake the prime out of your pan and put your musket down on the ground!"

The first three did as I told them to but the fourth man hesitated.

"Mister, you aint going to kill us, when our guns are unloaded, are you?"

"No, we aint British."

I thought for sure that he was going to change his mind and try to get away but the other men told him to do as he was told. He did. When the last musket was on the ground, I motioned to the man who had done the talking, the one in front and he rode up to me.

"Who are you and what made you want to stop being with the

British?"

"My name is Lewis Jackson. There were seven of us. We were paroled after Charlestown fell. We went home and were just glad to get out of the fighting. We didn't draw any attention until late January. We'd just heard about Tarleton getting his tail kicked at the Battle of the Cowpens, when British and Tories rode up to my farm. They said that because we were paroled, we had to fight for the king. One man, Ezekiel, refused and they hung him from a tree in front of his cabin and made his wife and young'uns watch. After that, nobody refused. We would have probably stayed but we saw British and some Tories treating some women just awful. The sixth man, Roger, tried to stop them and they killed him. The rest of us lit out and don't want to have nothing else to do with the British."

I kept my eyes on him, staring at him. He looked ashamed and couldn't look at me. He didn't know it but I was thinking of my sister-in-law. His saying that the British and Tories had treated women 'just awful' had brought it all back. I started getting mad. I knew that getting mad wouldn't help and might cause me to do something without thinking it through.

"How much fighting did you do for the British?"

"None. They sent us out stealing food but we didn't do any fighting for them."

"No fighting?"

"No fighting, thank goodness."

"Rob, tie these redcoats on the same horse and take them back to General Greene."

"What are you going to do."

"I'm going to check on a farm. We'll be along."

I turned back to the freshly surrendered men. I thought about it for a minute then decided that I'd use them.

"Rob, hand me the courier's pistols. You five, pick up your muskets but don't prime them yet."

Rob handed me the two pistols and I checked to make sure they were loaded. We waited until Rob had the couriers tied to one horse and headed through the woods, leading the extra horse. I turned to the others.

"Are you willing to go back and tackle the patrol that was treating the women awful?"

As I expected, the man who was in front answered for all of them, "I will." The others nodded.

"You lead."

He led. The others waited until he was moving then fell in behind him. I rode in the rear. After riding almost two miles, they stopped. The leader dismounted and tied his horse to a sapling. The others followed his example. I looked around before dismounting but I did and tied my horse to a sapling. I made sure both pistols and my musket were still primed and nodded at the men.

"Lewis, what do we have here?"

"Maybe twenty feet ahead, we'll be able to see the farm. We'll know then if the patrol is still there."

"Then you and me need to ease up and check."

Lewis motioned for the others to stay and we went to the edge of the brush. The saddled horses tied in a fenced lot and eating grass seemed to say that the patrol was still there. I spent a few minutes looking the whole area over and came up with an idea.

"There's nine horses. I take that to mean there's nine soldiers?"

"Yes, there's six British and three Tories."

"Are the Tories willing Tories or were they forced like you were?"

"Willing."

"Why don't they have guards posted?"

Lewis grinned and pointed at the other four men.

"You men are the guards?"

He nodded and grinned again.

"You got any ideas?"

"Ambush them when they leave?"

"What about we send three men up to take the horses?"

"Could do."

"Pick three men. Do it!"

Lewis went back to the other four men and talked for a couple of minutes. Three of them untied their horses and rode toward the farm. While they rode toward the farm, we took up a position that we could help them out with our muskets if help were needed.

The men rode to the gate and stopped. A British soldier walked toward them. After some talk, he shrugged and pointed toward the gate that opened to the lot where the horses were tied. The three men rode into the lot, glanced toward the house, then each took the ropes of three horses. The rode through the gate at a fast walk. When someone shouted from the house, the fast walk changed to a fast canter.

Three British soldiers and three Tory militiamen ran out of the house, carrying muskets. I raised my musket, Aimed at the top of their heads and shot. It was a long shot for a musket but the six were so close together that I was sure that I would probably hit one of them. I did. One of the British soldiers dropped his musket, then stumbled and fell. The other five rushed back inside. By the time they were inside, the three riders leading nine horses were hidden by the brush.

We waited about fifteen minutes before a white flag was waved out the doorway.

"One of you come on out"

A British sergeant carrying the flag walked out.

I walked out toward him. When he was about twenty-five paces from me, I called out, "I think that's close enough! What can I do for you?"

"If you surrender, we'll see that you're paroled and out of the war."

I pretended to think it over. I figured that since the threat of the Swamp Fox had worked once, it might work again.

"What makes you think that the Swamp Fox is interested in surrendering?"

"The Swamp Fox is over on the Pee Dee."

"He was. He aint. He's joined General Greene. If you choose to surrender, you'll leave here alive."

"Help will come for us."

"Will it come before the three militia with you decide to change sides again? You do know that they were Patriot militia before Charlestown fell. What makes you think they won't change sides again?"

"Bloody rebels!"

"It's really all up to you. Do you really think the militia won't save themselves by attacking you?"

"I trust you will continue to honor the flag of truce until I return inside."

"Sure, you're only concern is whether the three militiamen have tied up your unwounded soldier and are waiting to shoot you when you get back inside."

The sound of a woman screaming came from the house. The British sergeant seemed startled and looked back over his shoulder.

"If you surrender, you're safe."

I could see that he was struggling. He didn't trust anyone from South Carolina or for that matter, any of the thirteen states. Furthermore, the British soldiers had made General Francis Marion, the Swamp Fox, a lot bigger and meaner than he is. I could tell that he'd rather kill me and feed me to dogs than surrender.

"Damn you rebel, I surrender."

"Call back to the house that you have surrendered and tell the men in the house that you surrendered and that they are to walk to us with your hands raised and no weapons."

He did as he was told and the five men left the house and came toward us. The wounded soldier was helped by two of his fellow soldiers.

"Lewis! Come here and bring some rope. Sergeant, tell your soldiers to come to us, one at a time."

The soldiers came to us one at a time. As each arrived, Lewis tied their hands and tied hobbles on their ankles. The man was then taken back into the brush and tied on a horse. We put three men on each horse and made sure they were tied on tight. We put the three militia on one horse with one British soldier. We put the Sergeant and the wounded soldier on the same horse.

Before we left, I checked with the house. The two women inside offered to take care of the captured British and Tories. I remembered what my sister-in-law had done and was tempted but I told them that General Greene needed to question them. I hinted that torture was involved with the questioning.

The older woman, I figured she was the younger woman's ma, tried to look like she was calm but I could tell that she angry. She had a cold anger that I didn't want to be close to when she let it loose. Her daughter showed hot anger but her ma's anger was a lot more dangerous.

"Mister, we'll walk out with you and see them off."

"You don't have to do that."

"We want to see them off."

We walked to the rest of the newly reformed patriots and the prisoner. The mother smiled a smile that didn't have much smile behind it and walked over to a horse with three Tories on it.

"Lemuel Walker, did you think I wouldn't recognize you?"

"What?"

"I know where you live and I know what your family is like. I'm going to tell your wife that you raped me."

With that, she drew a small axe from the folds of her skirts and smashed the blade into his knee. Before anyone could reach her, she buried it in the knee again. Then, smiling sweetly, she and her daughter began walking back to their house.

After a few steps, she turned and called over her shoulder, "I know where you other Tories live and will talk to your wives too."

We bandaged the injured knee as tightly as we could. We stopped the bleeding but I figured he would lose the leg.

The British sergeant ranted and raved that the two women must be killed immediately. I ignored him.

We started to ride back to General Greene's camp as it was getting close to dusk. The sergeant kept looking around. He finally asked, "General Marion, where is he?"

"Back somewhere along the Pee Dee, I reckon."

The sergeant cursed me until I gagged him with a sleeve I cut from his shirt.

Four miles later, one of the Tories called me over to their horse. I could see that Lemuel was in bad shape.

"Mister, we got to get Lemuel some help. The pain will kill him."

"Do you reckon it will make you Tories more careful about abusing women?"

"We didn't know that she knew us."

"You know now."

I studied about how stupid men could act when they thought nobody knew them. I hoped that I would never be that stupid.

"About a mile and a half northwest, there's a farm that patriots live on. We could get him help there."

"What's the name of the people?"

"Delaney."

I rode over to Lewis and told him that Lemuel was in bad shape. He shrugged then told me, "I think the Delaney farm is close, Delaney is a good man."

"Let's go there then."

Going across brush and hills, it was at least a mile and a half, maybe closer to a little over two miles. It took us over an hour to get there. I knew we were close when a pack of dogs started barking. Lewis rode close to the house and called out to the house. The third time he called, A man called out of a window, "Lewis, are you a Patriot again or are you still a worthless Tory?"

"Always been a Patriot Matt, just don't want to be a hung patriot if I can help it."

"Who are you with?"

"Five Patriots and nine captives, one bad wounded."

"The captives tied real good?"

"Tied real good."

"Tie them in the hay shed. There's enough hay left to keep them comfortable. Better gag them so they can't call out. We get Tory riders sometimes. Bring the wounded one to the house and we'll tend to him."

We moved the prisoners to the hay shed and made sure they were tied real good and gagged so they couldn't call out. I tried to make sure they were as comfortable as a tied and gagged man could be but beyond that I wasn't too concerned. We tied our horses in an orchard behind the house and took all the prisoners weapons and ammunition with us. I figured the least we could do would be to give one to Matt for his trouble.

We carried Lemuel to the house and were met on the front step by Matt and his wife. His wife carried bandages and Matt carried a jug.

Matt's wife showed more concern that anyone else there. From the way she looked at us, I soon figured it out that she held us responsible for Lemuel's wounded knee. That didn't last too long.

She removed the bandages that we had put on his knee and glared at all of us. "Why was this necessary?"

"Well, he raped a woman and her daughter and the woman thought it was the proper thing to do."

"Raped?"

"Raped."

She dropped the bandages, picked up the jug and poured whiskey on the wounded knee. Lemuel screamed when the whiskey hit the open wounds. She turned and walked back into the house. Lemuel screamed until he was too hoarse to scream. Matt gave him a large drink of whiskey and wrapped his knee.

"Get me some splints."

His son came out of the cabin with some pieces of kindling wood and Matt placed the kindling around the knee and tied them in place with the rest of the bandages.

"Lemuel, if I was guessing, I'd guess that my woman don't like the idea of raping a woman and her daughter."

We sat in the front of the house and shared the whiskey. It was beginning to get dark and I was enjoying the cooler air. I had one small drink and Lewis had about the same amount. He also made sure the other four with him were served the same amount.

I was enjoying the shade and the whiskey when Matt's pack of dogs jumped up all at once and began loud barking. Matt jumped up too.

"Into the house! Quick!"

We went into Matt's house and waited. We took all the weapons and ammunition with us. I was afraid that we might need it soon. It took a few minutes before a dozen armed men carrying torches rode up to the door. The leader called out, "Matt, we hear you got some rebels here. Better give them up!"

I knew we were in big trouble. Fire could kill all of us including Matt and his family. I didn't want Matt's family hurt or the choice would have been easy. Fight! With Matt's family maybe having to pay a price, the choice wasn't as easy. Lemuel made the choice for me. While the Tories were shouting, Lemuel shouted back, "In the hay shed! In the hay shed!"

Of course, Lemuel was trying to tell them that his friends were prisoners in the hay shed but the Tories didn't take it that way. They rode to the shed and all their torches were thrown on, in and around the shed. The hay caught fire and as the fire quickly spread, the prisoners inside screamed through their gags. Hearing the screams, the Tories shot into the shed at the sound of the screams. Lemuel might have tried to warn them again but Matt's wife busted his head with a shovel.

While the Tories were having fun burning the shed and killing their comrades in arms, we loaded all the British Brown Bess's with buck and ball. This is a load of eight buckshot and one .72 Lead ball. Matt cut five loopholes in the wall. When the shed and the prisoners were destroyed, the Tories rode up to the door.

"Come on out Matt!"

Matt didn't go out. Instead, eight Brown Bess muskets came out of doors, windows, and loopholes. In seconds, sixty-four buckshot and eight round balls went into the mass of Tories. The volley was followed by screaming horses and Tories. Tories were on the ground screaming and trying to hold their insides in. I felt sorry for the horses. Using our own weapons, we finished the Tories who still showed fight. I felt sorry for their horses. Four horses were still healthy and we caught and tied them.

We led the horses who were too wounded to survive away from the house and killed them to stop their misery. Eight Tories were dead and four badly wounded. Their leader was one of the wounded. We led them to the coals and flames that had been a shed holding hay and stopped. I turned to the Tory leader and asked him, "Tory, what do you think of the damage done here?"

"Just rebels."

"They were six British soldiers and two Tories, and you murdered them."

"What?"

"I'm turning all of you over to the British at Camden. They will take care of you for murdering British soldiers."

They were tied but they tried to run. Lewis and his men made sure they didn't get far. Now we would have a lot of men to bury the next morning. It was close to midnight by the time we got things settled down. We couldn't do anything about the corpses in what had been the hay shed because the coals and fire were still too hot for us to deal with.

We posted guards all night. At first light, we went outside to begin burying the dead British and Tories. We stayed two days trying to help Matt begin building a new shed and cleaning up the mess. Matt's wife was left to care for Lemuel. He died.

We finally rode to where General Greene's army had been. It wasn't there. We finally found Greene's army in Camden - - - or what was left of Camden. I found Rob and Anne and they brought me up on what had happened.

Rob's story

On the night of May 7th, Colonel Rawdon crossed the Wateree Ferry and moved to attack Greene's force at Sandy Creek. He wasted his effort because all he found were the Light Infantry and cavalry pickets of the American army. All of our American forces were able to escape.

The next day, General Greene moved our army to Sandy Creek (some folks call it Sawhney's Creek). We arrived and found out that Rawdon had gone back to Camden. The next morning, Rawdon marched his army to Wateree Ferry. He followed General Greene to the lower side of Sandy Creek. This was a rough area of pine and oak trees. His advance guard met Colonel Washington's dragoons doing picket duty. A short fight started right off and the British drove our pickets back. The fight was short but hard. This time, Rawdon found out that he couldn't get any advantage on General Greene.

Rawdon pulled back his army before he lost any more men. Rawdon probably thought he was lucky to get back to Camden without losing his army. I guess he didn't want any more fights with General Greene's army so he ran back to Camden.

After leaving the fight at Sandy's Creek, Rawdon figured it was time to leave Camden. He destroyed everything he couldn't take with him. He released all the prisoners. He burned the jail. He burned the local mills. He burned many private homes. He burned all the supplies he couldn't take with him. He left Camden in ruins. He took the sick who could still travel and moved his army toward Charlestown. By May 10th, the British were out of Camden and General Greene moved his army into Camden the next day.

Colonel Rawdon left thirty-one wounded Patriot soldiers and fifty-eight of his own wounded men behind. The Tories in Camden left with Colonel Rawdon for Charlestown.[3]

---

[3] Lord Rawdon, in his letter of May 24th to Lord Cornwallis wrote: *"Whilst, upon that principle, I waited for my expected succours, Gen. Greene retired from our front, and, crossing the Wateree, took a position behind Twenty-five Mile Creek. On the 7th of May, Lieutenant-colonel Watson joined me with his detachment, much reduced in number through casualties, sickness, and a reinforcement which he had left to strengthen the garrison at George Town. He had crossed the Santee near its mouth, and had recrossed it a little below the entrance of the Congaree. On the night of the 7th, I crossed the Wateree at Camden ferry, proposing to turn the flank and attack the rear of Greene's army, where the ground was not strong, though it was very much so in front. The troops had scarcely crossed the river, when I received notice that Greene had moved early in the evening, upon getting information of my being reinforced, I followed him by the direct road, and found him posted behind Sawney's creek. Having driven in his pickets, I examined every point of his situation; I found it every where so strong, that I could not hope to force it without suffering such loss as must have crippled my force for any future enterprise; and the retreat lay so open for him, I could not hope that victory would give us any advantage sufficiently decisive to counterbalance the loss. The creek (though slightly marked in the maps) runs very high into the country. Had I attempted to get round him, he would have evaded me with ease; for, as his numbers still exceeded mine, I could not separate my force to fix him in any point, and time (at this juncture most important to me) would have been thus unprofitably wasted. I therefore returned to Camden the same afternoon, after having in vain*

By May 10th, the British were now out of Camden, and the next day, Major General Nathanael Greene moved in.

I found it a good thing that Lord Rawdon left thirty-one of our wounded Patriot soldiers behind. Of course, he also left fifty-eight of his own men, including three officers, who were too badly wounded to travel. The Tories were all afraid they would be held to account for all the meanness they had done to Patriots so they joined Lord Rawdon on his march to Charlestown.

---

attempted to decoy the enemy into action, by affecting to conceal our retreat."

5

Camp Follower Gossip

May 15, 1781

Once again, I went to listen to Rob and Ann to find out what was going on. I used to think that me and Dan could figure out what was happening just from our spying. Now Dan was in Virginia and now I was finding that, without him, I wasn't as sure of my opinions. Dan and me, we had started our spying coming east to whip Ferguson on King's Mountain. There were about a thousand of us, all militia volunteers. Now, because I had the reputation as a top spy, I was spying for General Greene and his army that on any day could have anywhere from a thousand to over three thousand Continental soldiers and militia. I was finding it was real different than just spying for Will Campbell, Jack Sevier and Ike Shelby.

Rob, his woman Anne and his mother-in-law were finishing up a load of laundry when I walked up. Rob looked a little put out when he saw that I caught him helping so I started to help but his mother-in-law didn't let me get too far.

"Nate Bowman! Don't you even think of getting your filthy hands on these clean clothes. They were hard enough to clean the first time without having to wash them again!"

"Yes ma'am."

I noticed that they were low on firewood so I went and gathered an arm load. I carried the wood back and sat down to wait. The clothes having been wrung as dry as they could get them were draped over some bushes to let the night breeze and morning sun finish drying them. Rob came to sit with me while the women cooked. I had found and killed three pigs that I found running wild. I brought the shoulder and loin of a pig with me and Rob's mother-in-law rigged a spit to roast the pork with.

Anne brought out some sassafras roots and started some tea, It looked like we might have a good feed for a change. Anne asked four of the other women to join us. I noticed that none of the women brought men with them. Rob's mother-in-law let me know that their husbands had been killed; two at Guilford Courthouse and two at Hobkirk's Hill.

I bowed my head toward the four widows and told them, "Ladies, I hope my wife is not in your position anytime soon."

I continued eating my supper and nothing else was said about the four women being widows. Instead, the women began talking about the army moving again.

"I aint sure that General Greene can whip the British."

The widow looked around to see if anyone disagreed. She didn't expect disagreement but I felt obliged to speak up.

"What do you think is wrong with General Greene?"

"Well, he aint won a battle yet. He didn't win at Cowan's Ford or Guilford Courthouse, or Hobkirk's Hill or anywhere else that I know of."

"You are partly right. He wasn't in charge at Cowan's Ford. He kept his army together after Guilford Courthouse and Hobkirk's Hill. He has kept this army, including camp followers supplied with rations. Rawdon just pulled his army back to Charlestown and he was glad to get away, I bet. His strategy is to keep as much of his army alive as he possibly can. I've find no fault with General Greene."

"Then why has he sent for General Sumter and General Marion?"

"Just smart, I reckon."

I hadn't been sure that Marion and Sumter had been sent for. I knew that Greene had sent for Sumter to join him at Hobkirk's Hill but Sumter had ignored the summons. I wasn't sure that Green would count on the South Carolina militia after that.

"So, Nate Bowman, where do you think that General Greene will go against next?"

"Where ever he wants but I'm thinking Ninety-Six."

"What's at Ninety-Six?"

"Colonel Cruger and a passel of British and Tories who are a long way from Charlestown."

"How'd it get a name like Ninety-Six?"

"I guess it depends on which liar you're hearing it from. The best that I heard is that it's exactly ninety-six miles from some Cherokee town or village."

"Will Greene be able to capture it?"

"Depends on how quick Ninety-Six gets reinforcements, how many militia show up and dozens of other what ifs. Greene is good but he knows that keeping his army together is important."

Two days later, Rob and me were spying out Ninety-Six. I'd been around it before but Rob never had. It didn't take long for both of us to know that it would be a tough nut to crack.

The village of Ninety-Six wasn't real big. It had been a village of fifteen buildings counting the courthouse and the jail. The British had built a wall around the town that protected over two acres. The British made Ninety-Six a base to operation after Charlestown was captured. Cornwallis thought Ninety-Six would be necessary to control the backcountry when the British Army moved north to Virginia and the Chesapeake. He left Cruger, in charge with orders to strengthen all fortifications and to do what was necessary to punish rebels and keep order. Cruger wasn't from England but was a Loyalist from New York. He used Ninety-Six as his headquarters and sent raids against local villages, militias and farms from there.

The British were feeling froggy and making big jumps until we whipped Ferguson on King's Mountain. Add to that whipping Tarleton at The Battle of the Cowpens, General Marion's hit and run attacks against the British in the low country while Sumter hit the British in the South Carolina up country and the British were getting concerned.

General Greene threw Cornwallis's plans into a whirlwind when he split his army and put General Morgan out to find British targets to pester. Ordinarily, Cornwallis would have gone after either Greene or Morgan with his whole army but this would have meant the army he wasn't going after could have attacked Ninety-Six.

When Morgan whipped Cornwallis's pet dog, Tarleton, at the Battle of the Cowpens, that was two victories in a row where the British weren't just defeated, they were whipped. Cornwallis claimed victory at Guilford Courthouse but while he held the field, his losses were worse than his army could afford. The same had occurred to Rawdon At Hobkirk's Hill. Rawdon had lost a fourth of his army either killed, wounded or captured.

Anne's widow friend was right in saying that Greene hadn't won any big victories but Rawdon had abandoned Camden having lit a shuck back to Charlestown. Light Horse Harry and the Swamp Fox had captured Fort Watson and Fort Motte. The chain of British forts that had once seemed so strong now seemed to be considerably weaker. It was no surprise to many that General Greene's next target was Ninety-Six. Of course, a lot of other people found fault with his decision.

While I sat with Rob, his wife and mother-in-law and the others, the crowd of camp followers started to get bigger. They didn't come all at once but by ones and twos. Then by threes and fours. What was a little surprising was how much of the information the women had right. Mind you, they didn't have all of it right but they had a right smart of it either right or pretty close.

One thing I learned there was that the women liked to talk. Every one of them had an opinion on everything and they all wanted to say what their opinion was. One of the widows that joined us had things pretty close to right. Not entirely but pretty close.

"We still don't have a bigger army than the British. Their army is like a mighty oak tree. Our militias are like a drawer full of little knives. None of our militia's big enough to cut down that mighty oak but they keep whittling at it. They done took a bunch of the limbs and branches off but they aint come close to putting it down yet. What they have done is pruned a lot of its strength - - - that is what every limb and branch is, strength. Before the dust settles, I'm sure that the mighty oak tree will be whittled bare of limbs and branches and be just a pole in the ground."

She turned to look at me like she was daring me to say different. I knew better to argue right off, so I just asked what her name was."

"Arlene, Arlene Caldwell."

"Well, Arlene, I admire the thought you've put in to it, and I reckon there's a right smart to what you got to say. The British do have us outnumbered. Our leaders like Marion and Sumter have whittled them away to the point that a bunch of their posts have already been deserted and the British headed either to Charlestown or somewhere else. I don't see how Ninety-Six and Augusta can stay manned."

I didn't tell them that we had caught a courier from Rawdon to Cruger at Ninety-Six, telling Cruger that he needed to leave Ninety-Six and hightail it to Augusta. I could see that Rob started to tell them but he saw me shake my head a bit and he didn't. He didn't have much time to say anything because Arlene began to talk again.

"Yes, and I heard tell that General Sumter wanted General Greene to take off after Rawdon and the British but now folks tell that General Greene is aiming to attack Ninety-Six. I can't for the life of me see why Greene don't take after Rawdon and whup him like a borrowed plow horse."

"Well, General Greene has a sight more to think about than we do. He has spies that give him a sight more news than we have. Since he's in charge and has all that responsibility, I reckon we should just let him alone to win the war down here."

I had already heard that Greene had written Governor Reed that the countryside around Ninety-Six, Camden and Augusta had been stripped bare of provisions and that no army could live on what the land there had to offer. It was just a matter of commonsense that, any post cut off from supplies, would have to evacuate or surrender. Any army coming to relieve those posts would have to bring a lot of supplies or do without because there were no supplies left in the countryside along the route.

Lord Rawdon had sent several messengers by different routes, and asked Colonel Balfour to send out the same messages to Colonel Cruger at Ninety-Six so Cruger would know what was going on. We had caught several of Rawdon's messengers. Like I said, I figured that Greene knew more than I did and was doing the best he could.

The other question was, why didn't Cruger try to evacuate to Augusta? The only answer I could come up with was that he knew that even united with the British at Augusta, they couldn't have made it to Savannah. He probably knew that militias were already in place to try to stop him from reaching Augusta and stationed between Augusta and Savannah as well. I didn't mention any of this and with no one talking, one of the women with Arlene spoke up.

"I hear that General Sumter wants to fight the British but that General Greene don't trust him none."

"That might be right, but you need to understand that Greene has to make his decisions based on what he knows. General Greene knows that last summer, General Sumter was surprised by Tarleton with a fourth the number of men that Sumter had and routed Sumter's command."

"Well, do you reckon that Greene just wants to leave South Carolina for Marion, Sumter and Pickens to tend to and go running off to Virginia?"

That was a possible answer. Greene was eager to go face to face with Cornwallis again. At Guilford Courthouse, he had moved his army from the battle when it was still a tossup, knowing that he had badly damaged Cornwallis's army without having damaged his as badly. Retaking Charlestown would be done but it was more a matter of driving all the British back to the city and bottling the British up in the city. Then, with luck, a French fleet could blockade the city from the Atlantic.

There was probably more honor to be gained in Virginia. If all the British strength moved that way to cut off everything from the Chesapeake south, it would be quite a fight. General Greene, after all, was the commander of the Southern Department and it might irk him that he was not in the thick of the struggle.

While the camp followers continued to voice their opinions, I gave it some thought. Greene might think that just running the British back to Charlestown wasn't enough. I'd heard him say that a siege required four times the number they were besieging. I wondered if the reason he was irritated with Sumter for not joining at Camden was because he didn't give Rawdon the whipping he could have with Sumter. I figured that a clear victory at Camden and he would have had an excuse to head north to Virginia. I was suddenly convinced that a clear victory at Ninety-Six would send him and his continentals heading north to Virginia.[4] Having studied about what Greene might do, I turned my attention back to the gossip of the camp followers. A woman that I think they called Helen was talking.

"I been told that when the Georgia militia went back to Georgia, they agreed to a place to meet, then they split up into bunches of ten or twelve and returned to their homes. When they got back home, they found that their fathers and brothers had been hung and any grandfathers there were had been put into a prison. Their mothers, wives, sisters, daughters, and young children had been robbed, done dirty and been insulted, and abused. They found them living in huts an Indian wouldn't have lived

---

[4] *When General Greene arrived at Ninety-Six, he wrote Lafayette "If we are successful here I shall move northwardly immediately with a part of our force if not all." That is, if Ninety-six fell, he would leave Sumter, Marion, and Pickens to contend with Rawdon.*

in. They began looking for the Tories who had done the wrongs and they didn't take prisoners and they didn't show no mercy neither. The Whig captains, Johnson and McKoy, gathered up what men they could find and just like our Swamp Fox, they went to the swamps along the Savannah river. They aim to attack the British and Tories between Augusta and Savannah. I heard they aim to stop them two places from sending messages back and forth too. I heard the British sent men after them and McKoy heard about it and ambushed them. They killed the officer in command and fifteen or twenty of his men. I heard them that was left lit out back to Augusta."

Some were looking at me to say something. I didn't want to even think about some of the things I'd seen or knew about, let alone talk about them. No one else was talking and I felt like they were looking at me so I figured that I needed say something.

"Helen, I sure hate to hear about the wrongs done to innocent people in Georgia."

Soon, another woman was talking. Lord a mercy, I don't know how they did it but these camp followers heard about things as quick as spies did. I wondered if the officers whose laundry they did talked too much and too careless.

"The British attacked a Colonel Harden down there. Harden got his men out of there without losing too many. I heard the British lost more. Just like the Swamp Fox does, he took them to an Island in the Savannah River to heal up. He got help and food from a man named Tanner. When this Tanner was took prisoner by Tories, they tortured and then murdered him because he wouldn't tell them where Harden's wounded were at. I heard that the Tories turned some prisoners over to Indians so the Indians could torture them. Those Tories and their Indians stripped the men and women, of their clothes and set fire to their houses."

Then Arlene Caldwell interrupted again.

Arlene's tale about Colonel Snipe

Colonel Snipes is a South Carolinian and he is knowed for his strength and bravery almost as much as he is knowed for his hatred of Tories. He hates Tories with a passion that burns with a bright flame. Like many of his friends and neighbors, he has lost property to Tories and has been injured by Tories. It is said that he would not allow himself to forgive Tories or forget the wrongs they had done to him and other patriots. When fighting the Tories, his temper would just take him over and he'd go wild. His treatment of the Tories was just like the treatment patriots had got from the devilish Tories. General Marion had to get on to Snipes more than once for the rough way he treated the Tories.

It was after a long spell of attacking supply caravans and fighting the British, Snipes returned to his plantation to rest and gather supplies to take back to General Marion. He did not return to his plantation by a direct route but by a wide and meandering path that he rode with caution. Some folks saw him traveling and reported to Tory leaders that Colonel Snipes was returning to his plantation. The Tories took to his trail with a large party and trailed him to his plantation. Snipes got to his plantation safely without knowing that Tories were trailing him.

They say that Snipes spent the day checking his property and seeing all that had been done while he was riding with the Swamp Fox. He took a report from Henry, his slave that he had left in charge, and relaxed with his slaves and talked with them about their needs. There having been no sign of trouble he went to sleep after having a good supper. Before midnight, he was woke up by his slave, Henry. Henry told him that Tories were coming.

Henry told him that armed Tories were closing in on the House. Snipes told Henry he was going to the barn to get a horse but Henry showed him that the barn was already afire. He was barely able to escape from his house in his night shirt with two slaves who Henry told to hide him. That's right, he had to leave the house, covered only by his night shirt, with two slaves. The slaves took him to a thicket about a hundred yards from the house and stayed with him.

Colonel Snipes protected by his Slave Henry,   Public Domain

The Tories surrounded his house and called for him to come out. Henry came out the front door and told the Tories that his master wasn't in the house. Of course, Colonel Snipes wasn't in the house. He was hidden in a thicket so thick with briars that his nightshirt had been ripped to shreds, leaving him almost naked. Snipes was bleeding from injuries as were the two slaves with him. He was injured but he was alive.

In front of the house, the Tories grabbed Henry and demanded to know where Colonel Snipes was hiding. They were too scared of Colonel Snipes to go inside his house lest he attack them in the darkness but they threatened to Kill Henry. While trying to beat Snipes whereabouts out of Henry. They surrounded the burning house with cocked muskets hoping to kill Snipes as he tried to escape. Snipes heard their shouts and saw his home burning but the two slaves with him, following Henry's orders, held him down and wouldn't let him call out. The house burned to the ground and the sight of the burning was a torture to Colonel Snipes and he had to be held tightly by the two slaves to prevent his charging the Tories.

When Snipes did not come out of the house, the Tories tried to torture Henry into telling them where Snipes was hiding. The Tories placed a noose around his neck threw the rope over a tree branch. Three times, they pulled Henry off the ground and demanded where Colonel Snipes was hiding. Three times he was choked to unconsciousness and three tomes he refused to tell where they might find Colonel Snipes. His ability to endure the torture was stronger than the will of the Tories to torture him. The Tories finally dropped Henry to the ground, unconscious.

The other slaves nursed Henry and he lived. Colonel Snipes sat up with Henry until morning.

The next morning, Colonel Snipes gathered up some militia and went after the Tory militia. It is said that he revenged himself and Henry upon the Tories who had attacked his home. No one ever said if General Marion rebuked Colonel Snipes from getting his revenge.

Fortunately, I didn't have to say anything because another camp follower jumped right into the conversation.

"Well that's something but I heard a tale worse than that. There's a widow name of Mrs. McKoy. This lady, a widow, had to run from her home at Darien in Georgia into South Carolina for safety from the Tories. Her oldest boy, just seventeen years old, was with the Patriot militia and was took prisoner. His ma heard about it and went right off to the Tory camp. She took some refreshments that gave to the Tory leader and begged him to spare her son as she was a widow. While the Tory ate the food, he turned her down and refused to even let her see her son. He had her forced out of camp. A Scottish officer was there and he tried to talk the tory into mercy but it wasn't any use. The

Tory had a pen built made of fence rails about three feet high. He placed his prisoners in it and had it covered over with fence rails. Mrs. McKoy, tried to see her son again but wasn't allowed in the camp. The Scottish captain wasn't allowed to talk to her and the next morning, her son was hung with a bunch of other Patriots."

I guess that gossip can travel quicker than a fast horse. Some of the women seemed to be both scared and excited by all the talk of British and Tory meanness. But, like I said, I had a lot of stuff I don't want to think about. No, I don't like to remember it and I sure don't want to talk about it.

I stood up and turned to Rob.

"Rob, I reckon that we better be ready to ride about an hour shy of first light."

"I'll be ready Nate."

5

New Plans

The next morning, before first light, I was walking up to Greene's headquarters area. Rob was behind me, leading our horses. I still wasn't as comfortable with Rob as I had been with Dan but I was getting more used to him.

General Greene was nowhere in sight but one of his aides, Major John Carter was waiting with two pouches. I stepped up to take them and asked, "Major Carter, which lies are most popular today?"

"You tell me. I've been too busy to listen."

"You can start by telling us what is in the message pouches."

"Why would you need to know?"

"If it comes down to us getting caught, we'll try to get rid of the pouches, in a fire if we can. Then, if we can, we'll still deliver the message by telling the message to the right person."

"Do you think there'll be a problem?"

"Hope not, but look at how many messages we took from British and Tory couriers. I don't want it to happen to us but we both know that it could. Besides, I got a pretty good notion of what the message will be."

"And just what do you think the message will be Nate Bowman?"

"I reckon that General Greene is telling Light Horse Harry and the Swamp Fox to meet him at Ninety-Six and help him take it."

"That was the message yesterday. You are taking them a message to ignore that message and to raise as much devilment as they can away from Ninety-Six. You will tell Colonel Lee to go help take Augusta. One of you will anyway. The other will be staying here to run messages back and forth between General Greene and Colonel Lee."

"Well, Rob, how do you feel about spying with the Swamp Fox for a spell?"

Rob looked so stricken that Major Carter and I both laughed. Given a choice, Rob would not want to get too far from his new bride, even if her mother was with her.

Rob took him a deep breath and let it out slow. "Nate, I reckon I'll go where the army needs me to go."

"Well, Rob, the army wants you to stay as close to your lovely mother-in-law as you can. I don't aim to have her aggravating me about you running off to gallivant all over the swamps with General Marion."

"Now Nate, I'll go where I'm needed. Where do you need me, Major Carter?"

Major Carter didn't answer at first but he finally nodded at us.

"You are to find General Marion and Lieutenant Colonel Lee and inform them General Marion is to raise the devil with the British to keep them occupies away from Ninety-Six and Augusta. You are to tell Lieutenant Colonel Lee that he is to proceed to Augusta in Georgia. We are attacking both forts."

"How long has the General been interested in Augusta?"

"A long time Nate. Some of the folks that think General Greene isn't doing enough, don't know everything that he has done. From the time he replaced Granny Gates, Greene had been encouraging Georgia Patriots to resist the British. He went so far as to send Continental soldiers toward Georgia to try to "spirit up" the Patriots. He tried to get Tories to change their allegiance by offering a better reconciliation policy. He had a Georgia Legion established to give the state to help build its government back up. He tried to work with the Georgia patriots instead of just bossing them."

"I know most of that. Why wasn't something done before?"

"I reckon that General Greene is one of the best when it comes to taking things that are messed up and putting them in order. Before being placed in charge of the American Southern command, he had taken the mess that was the Quartermaster Department and made it work. Despite doing a bang-up job with the Quartermaster Department, Greene was tickled to death to leave it all behind and get back to being with the real army. I've been an aide for General Greene since before he got to North Carolina and I find him to be a smart man with a lot of common sense. He is careful not to tramp on the people serving beneath him and he pays more attention to the little things than any man I can think of does."

"I've got to agree with that."

I don't think that Carter heard me. He was looking past me and maybe into himself. He went on talking and I went on listening.

"General Greene has something else that I have trouble describing. The best way I can put it is that he looks to see what something we do today will cause to happen next week or next year. Robert Howe, Benjamin Lincoln, and Horatio Gates had not been able to work with the Georgia Patriots or get their confidence but General Nathaniel Gates has been able to do just that. No sooner had General Greene got to Charlotte in December 1780, than he saw the problem in Georgia and started to fix it."

I was certain that Carter wasn't ready to shut up so I wasn't ready to stop listening. I stayed quiet and let him go on talking.

"There's been fighting in Georgia by Georgia Patriots for quite a while. The British beat off an attack on Savannah by French and Americans in 1779. The British at Augusta beat off an attack by a bunch of back-country patriots led by Elijah Clark in 1780. From the week that General Green had got to Charlotte, he had started talking to Deputy Paymaster Joseph Clay about what was needed in Georgia. When Greene found out that Colonel Few had been doing a good job mustering Georgia refugees in the Long Cane district, he wrote Few and encouraged him to keep on doing a good job. He also warned him to be on guard against surprise attacks. One thing is for sure, General Greene was determined to bring order to the back country of Georgia and the Carolinas."

Carter looked at me so I nodded at him. He nodded back and went right on a talking.

"This was a troubling time. The Tories were stealing, plundering, and attacking homes of Patriots. The natural thing for people do who had been wronged in such a manner is to hit back the same way. Greene thinks that such actions should not be done to retaliate while the people are deciding whether they want to follow the British or our side. A choice of two opinions. The two opinions are, of course, Patriot or Tory. General Greene told General Daniel Morgan to give support the actions and spirit up the people of the back country."

Carter stopped, rubbed face with his left hand, smiled and went on talking.

"Greene's decision to split his army and send Morgan to west of the Catawba River was a real smart move. Cornwallis just didn't know how to act or what to do. Cornwallis was camped where he would be able to attack either part of Greene's army but Cornwallis couldn't attack without Ninety-Six and Augusta open to an attack by the other part of the army. I reckon that Cornwallis figured he had no choice except to do what he done which was turn Tarleton loose so he could get his tail kicked at the Cowpens. While Greene's men kept Cornwallis in a bind, the British at Augusta were trying to talk the Cherokee into taking to the warpath against Patriots in the mountain country. The British figured that the Indians would aggravate the mountain people living in the back country and keep the Patriot militias from attacking Tories in North and South Carolina. They might have been right."

"They might have been Major Carter."

Yes, Brown who is commanding at Augusta, bragged that he had Indians who could take messages all the way from Florida to Quebec. He also bragged that he had Indians bringing him captives, usually women and children. He also bragged of his intention of raising Tory militia to attack Patriot militia and women and children in the backcountry of the Carolina's."

"Any man who would do that should be horse whipped to death!"

"Maybe so. Before Greene had been in Command a month, General Daniel Morgan's cavalry attacked a bunch of Brown's Tories in the Ninety-Six district. Morgan reported that the Tories were insulting and plundering the Patriots there. Colonel Will Washington chased the Tories to a place called Hammond's Store House and whipped them like dusty rugs. This caused Cornwallis to send the arrogant braggart Banastre Tarleton to stop Morgan. Morgan was seriously thinking about going all the way to Georgia to spirit up the people. Morgan wanted to stay on the attack so that militias would continue to join him. Morgan figured that if he seemed to retreat, local militias would think he was losing and join the British. Elijah Clark's men led by John Cunningham and Jim Jackson joined Morgan in time to fight with him at the Battle of the Cowpens and share the glory of victory. Clark was recuperating from a wound received at a place called Long Cane."

"I heard about that."

Now, of course, I'd heard about it. Me and Dan had been there. I could have told him a thing or two about it but I learned a long time ago that I learned more by listening than talking.

"Nate, after Morgan's whipped Tarleton's hind end, things began to change. Victory over Tarleton was changed a whole lot of things. For instance, Brown's Cherokee friends started to wonder if siding with the British was a good idea. I don't reckon that the Cherokee will join the British. Morgan's victory has encouraged the Georgia Patriots to try to drive the British out. They've been doing a good job of it too. Yes indeed, they have been doing a pretty good job of it. While General Greene led Cornwallis into North Carolina and toward Virginia, a Rebel Army of the ragged, tired, rough militiamen who followed Andrew Pickens aggravated the British in South Carolina and Georgia. Their actions caused other militias to be raised and to aggravate the British even more. For these and a lot of other reasons, Greene decided to let Pickens leave Greene's army and return to threaten the posts at Ninety-Six and Augusta."

"So now, General Greene is sending me to light a fire under the Swamp Fox and Light Horse Harry."

"That's exactly what he is doing."

"I gather that we're going to keep right on a stinging the British no matter where they're at or what they're a doing."

"Are you asking or stating?"

"Both, I reckon."

"You're awful curious for a messenger."

"Major Carter, I've been doing this since before Ramseur's Mill in June last year. Before that, I was busy fighting off Tories and protecting my kin and neighbors. While I'm toting messages, I'm spying. The more I know, the more I know what to spy for."

"That sounds reasonable. We're going to sting them at so many places, they won't know where to swat. Just the other day, General Sumter captured Orangeburg."

I'd heard something."

"Well, Sumter took Orangeburg. He captured the British post with all its garrison of British Regulars and some Tories too.

"How did he do it?"

General Greene gave him a 6-pound cannon. General Sumter used the cannon to attack the British garrison at Orangeburg. The British commanding officer there was Captain Henry Giesendanner. He had a lot of help there, seventy or so regulars and fifteen Tory militia.

General Sumter took over a hundred men and went to

Orangeburg ahead of the cannon. They lay a siege and the British took cover in a big brick building. The British sent out messages to Charlestown asking for help but they didn't get any. We captured all their messengers, at least I think we did. Maybe one got through but it didn't matter. The British in Charlestown didn't send him any help. When Sumter got his cannon, he commenced using it on the brick house. It didn't take long before he'd knocked a hole through the gable end of the house. He kept his cannon pounding and pretty soon, there were more holes and the British raised a white flag. Sumter had the British captain in charge tossed in the town's jail."

"I'm glad to hear that Sumter did that."

"That isn't all. We just heard a rumor that Lieutenant Colonel Lee forced Fort Granby to surrender."

That was news I hadn't heard. "When did this happen?"

"No more than two days ago. Lee and his Legion hit the fort and overwhelmed the British and Tories there. The rumor we got said that he put his 6-pounder about 400 yards from the fort before first light. As soon as the morning fog was burned off, Lee had the cannon fired and he fired his cannon. While the cannon was being fired, Lee moved up his infantry and they advanced on the fort. Lee got them within musket range, they stopped and fired a volley. After the volley, Lee asked the British in fort Granby to surrender."

"That sounds easy."

"Not as easy as it sounds. The British commander said they would only surrender if they could keep all the goods and property they had stolen during the past month or so. Lee had heard that Colonel Francis, Lord Rawdon would be there real soon so he agreed but told the British that he wanted all the horses the garrison had. The British cavalry and mounted infantry raised cane about that and negotiations came to a quick stop. Then Colonel Lee heard that Rawdon had crossed the Santee River and was on his way to reinforce the post so he agreed to the terms that the British wanted. So, the 'defeated' British marched out with their artillery, a large amount of baggage, and all the loot they had stolen from the countryside.

Colonel Lee took all the supplies left and ordered the fort burned. He captured 192 muskets, 86 bayonets, 63 rifles, 8,928 musket cartridges, 100 cartridge boxes, around 3,000 flints, and over 120 pounds of powder, over 325 pounds of lead, twenty 12-pound canister shots, and one drum."

"Could have been worse, could have been better."

"While Lee was stinging them at Fort Granby, Elijah Clarke and the Georgia militia laid a whipping of Colonel Tom Brown and his Tories."

"How bad?"

"Bad enough! Clarke and his Georgia Patriots whipped a bunch of the Kings Rangers commanded by Colonel Tom Brown. The report we just got said that a lot of the Tories were killed. Brown had to retreat."

7

Mission to Marion

It was still shy of first light when I rode out of camp east toward General Marion and his militia. I was being watchful and careful. I wasn't so much worried about British patrols as I was worried about Tory militia. The Tories still believed that no matter what happened, the British would finish on top and they would be able to take whatever they wanted, be it livestock, property or even whole plantations.

One thing you couldn't say about Tories is that they were shy about being greedy. Mindful of that, I tried to travel on paths and off the main roads. I was riding one horse and leading a second one. Every hour, I'd switch horses and let them drink and graze while I switched the saddle and bridle. This gave me a chance to stretch too.

Traveling from before light till dark, I covered over forty miles before I stopped. I had the name and location of some places I could stop and I rode right into one.

Of course, I smelled the smoke before I got too close. I slowed down and started whistling. I still think that I surprised the sentry a little bit.

"Stop right there!"

I stopped and waited.

"I said stop!"

"I am stopped. I need to speak to the man in charge. I have messages."

"Who do you think is in charge?"

"Tillery is who I was told."

"Well he aint. We voted him out. He had too many ideas about drilling and such."

"Who is in charge?"

"Uh, nobody, we aint voted yet."

"When are you going to vote?"

"We aint decided yet."

"Well, while you're deciding, I'm going to rub down my horses and tend to them. Then I need some food because it's been a long time since I ate and I need to talk to the folks that think they are running this outfit."

"I aint sure I'm supposed to let you go."

"You better make up your mind quick. I aim to go and I done see that you don't have a flint in your frizzen."

While he jerked his musket around to check the flint, I grabbed the barrel and twisted it hard and sudden. The sentry squawked and I pulled the musket away from him.

"Hellooooo the camp!"

"Who's helloing over there Brad?"

"I don't know but he just stole my gun!"

"He what!"

"He just stole my gun!"

"Who is he?"

The sentry, I could see now that he was no more than about fourteen, turned toward me and asked, "I – I, just who are you mister?"

"I'm Nate Bowman."

"Hey John, he says he is Nate Bowman!"

"Who is he carrying messages from?"

"Mister, who …."

"I heard him."

I kneed my horse and walked it to the middle of eighteen or twenty militiamen. I stripped the saddle and bridle and tied both horses where there was water and grazing. When they were taken care of and wiped off, I turned to face the militiamen.

"Where is Jed Tillery"

"He aint in charge no more."

"You fool, I didn't ask if he was in charge. I asked where he's at. Where is he."

"He said he was going to stay at home until we told him he's in charge again."

"Then somebody better go tell him he's back in charge. I can tell that none of you can do it."

"You don't know nothing. I'm a natural leader! It's just that these others are jealous and won't follow me."

I had to stare at the speaker for a good two or three minutes to figure out that he was serious.

"Tell me what your name is."

"It's Gerald. My name is Gerald Vance."

"Well Gerald, pick someone to go with you and go fetch Tillery. You, you, and you," I pointed at three militiamen, "I want you on picket duty now. If we get hit tonight, I want some warning. The rest of you, make sure your muskets are clean and loaded. Everyone will get guard duty before morning. Now move!"

Everyone moved and did as they were told. It's a good thing too because I was too tired to travel any further and I didn't aim to stay if they couldn't or wouldn't straighten up.

I made sure my horses were brushed down good and managed to find some grain for them. They had had a long, rough day and had more to come. Just under two hours after Gerald Vance left, he returned with his riding companion and two other men.

"Nate Bowman, I brought him back."

"About time! Step down and step over here Tillery."

"What about me Nate?"

I knew the voice but I couldn't put a name or a face to it. As he walked with crutches toward me, I could see that he was wounded or injured. I finally figured out who he was.

"Is that you Tom?"

"It's me Nate."

"What are you doing out here?"

"Fetching messages to General Marion. At least I was till I busted my ankle. The message will be late now."

"What is the message?"

"General Greene wants the Swamp Fox to join him to attack Ninety-Six."

"Then late is not a problem. Greene is sending me to tell Marion not to pay any attention to the message you're carrying."

"That makes it easy on both of us."

"Yes, it does. Can you ride?"

"Yes, but only short trips."

The story of what happened to Tom taken care of, I turned to Tillery and asked him, "Tillery, what in the world happened here?"

"The men with good sense left to work their farms and spend time with their wives. These youngsters decided that they didn't join the militia to pull guard duty, practice drill and the ordinary stuff. Every one of them joined to loaf and to be in charge."

"I kind of caught that. The one named Vance told me that he was a natural leader but the others wouldn't follow him because they were jealous."

"Most of them think that way."

"How long has this been going on?"

"Since the last bunch went home and their younger brothers or sons took their turn. Most of these men - - - and I say men reluctantly - - - have never been in a serious fight with either the British or the Tories. They're all eager to lead others to a big victory. They just don't know or aint willing, to do the work it takes."

"If they don't learn to post sentries and keep their muskets ready, their first fight will be pretty one-sided, with them getting whipped."

"I hope they learn. Maybe they'll listen now."

"It might help if we give them a taste of something tomorrow. Do you have anybody that needs pestering or have you got any news about the British moving supplies anywhere?"

"I know where we might find a Tory who rides with Cunningham and his bunch. He usually has half a dozen or so Tories with him."

"I think you should go tell the man that they have a dangerous mission to go on tomorrow. Give them something to think about."

"Good idea."

Tillery stood and walked toward the men who weren't on sentry duty. He spoke to them for ten minutes. As Tillery walked away, the men began to pay serious attention to their muskets and equipment.

After a little talk with Tillery, I turned in to sleep. Tillery woke me about two hours before daylight and handed me a cup something that was close to coffee. Twenty minutes later, we were riding.

Bloody Bill Cunningham was a strong and violent man. Those

who know him say that he is a brave man but his bloodthirsty acts make him appear to be a bully and a coward. When the war started in 1775, Cunningham enlisted as a private soldier in Colonel Thomson's Regiment of Rangers in the service of the State of South Carolina in Capt. John Caldwell's company. He was to be promoted but some offense cancelled the promotion and he was sentenced to be whipped.

Cunningham was forced to take the punishment but they couldn't force him to like it. After the whipping, he deserted and fled to Florida. He would have stayed there except that word reached him that his father was kicked out of his house by a man named Will Richie. Cunningham took his rifle and returned to South Carolina. He walked from St. Augustine with his rifle and killed Will Richie in his own home in front of his family.

While in South Carolina, he was offered command of a Tory militia . . . all he had to do was raise the company of militia. He did. With his company of mounted Tories, he became the most merciless Tory hellhound in the Carolinas. He searched the country, and hunted to their death, Carolina patriots.

Bloody Bill's men were like their leader. Men like Will Parker, Henry Parker, Will Kilmer, Jon Kilmer, Hall Foster, Jesse Gray, Will Dunahox, Isaac, Aaron, and Curtis Mills, Ned and Dick Turner, Matthew Love, Bill Elmore, Hubbles, John Hood, Fred Bell, and Moultrie. They, like Bloody Bill, liked to get revenge when their victims were helpless. Bloody Bill went to the home of his old commander Major John Caldwell, already retired from the militia. He found the man sitting in his own house, without shoes or stockings. Bloody Bill stamped on his toes and kicked his shins. Before leaving, he told him that this was revenge for the whipping he got serving in the Major Caldwell's command.

Bloody Bill took delight in talking patriots into surrendering with the promise of parole, then murdering them. He seemed to particularly like to kill men he had known before the war, especially those who had been his friends.

Fred Bell was one of Bloody Bill's lieutenants who was just as bloodthirsty as his leader. He had sent a message that found its way to Tillery that he wanted to talk about surrendering and turning in his leader. Of course, Tillery knew that Bloody Bill had used this same ruse to capture and murder patriots. He also discovered that Fred Bell was with his men at a tavern.

We got to the tavern later than we had aimed to get there but it was raining and the rain slowed us up. It also kept the Tories inside the tavern. Tillery kept the militia back where he could tell them what he wanted done and sent me ahead to spy out the tavern.

I was watching when four men left the tavern and relieved four others on sentry duty. Two sentries were posted in a shed and two in the barn. I figured from their staggering that the new sentries had woke up with heads busted from too much ale or other spirits the night before and had tried to solve the problem with more spirits for their breakfast.

The four sentries who had been relieved didn't look much better. I saw one of the old sentries hand a jug to his relief sentry. It looked like an easy place to attack but I stayed hidden in the trees and watched. After about half an hour, a woman came out with four baskets. She took a basket to the shed, then three baskets to the barn. A rope dropped from an opening and she tied two baskets to the rope. The baskets were pulled up to the hay loft.

I watched a little longer. While I watched, a man rode up and entered the tavern. I returned to Tillery. He was keeping the militiamen close under the trees where there was a little shelter from the rain. The militiamen had been trying to talk tiller into attacking the tavern and getting it over with.

"What did you find Nate?"

"Trouble. Is every man we started with still here?"

Tillery did a head count then asked, "Where is Dan Mills?"

The men looked at each other, then one answered, "Dan had to go to the bushes, his stomach was bothering him."

"Tillery, a man riding a grey horse just rode up to the tavern."

"You men, what color of horse was Dan riding?"

After a minute of confusion, they decided it was a light colored horse but that it was hard to tell because the horse was wet. Tillery turned to me and I think he knew the answer before he asked the question.

"Nate, what do you think."

"I think that if we go, we'll be riding into an ambush."

"We can try to ride around the ambush or we can decide not to attack. If we decide not to attack, then we can wait here to be attacked or we can leave this place."

"That's the way I see it."

Tillery told his men what was going on and that we would be leaving. After losing sleep and riding in the rain for hours, none of them liked it but most had enough sense to agree. Some didn't.

Gerald Vance and four other men got on their horses and Gerald told the others, "I don't aim to run, I aim to attack! Them that aint cowards, come on!"

Seven of them left, running their horses toward where the tavern stood. Tillery cussed then turned to the militia that was left.

"Men, check your prime and keep it dry. We'll try to save those fools but we need to make sure we save ourselves while we're at it."

Tillery took half the men and they rode the same direction that Vance had rode. I took the rest and we arced around at a faster pace. Half way there, we heard gunfire at the tavern. By the time we got there, three of the attackers were dead and the other four were captured.

I could feel the stares of the six men with me but I was busy watching the wood line directly in front of the tavern. While I watched, four ropes were thrown over the ridge pole of the barn. There were ten Tories in front of the barn. I thought there might still be some in the hay loft.

I pointed to two men. "You two hold fire but aim your muskets at the front of the loft where they load the hay in. The rest of you pick a target on the ground. When I say three, shoot. One, two three . . . "

The four men shot and two Tories fell. Not too bad considering the range. Before the echoes died, the Tories were shooting back. No shots came from the shed but four men crowded the hay loft opening ready to shoot. Then my other two men shot and two of the five men crowded together in the opening fell. The five of them made too big a target to miss, even with muskets.

The Tories turned their attention on us while the militiamen tried to reload. I still had my rifle and it was still loaded.

"Steady men, get your loads right."

I aimed at the man who seemed to be in charge of the Tories and touched off a shot. The Tory fell and the others showed a bit of confusion. Then Tillery and his bunch fired into the Tories. Two fell and it looked like two others had been hit.

That was enough for them. Five grabbed horses that Vance and his men had been riding. The three left in the loft were on their own.

Our only casualties were the three with Vance who had been killed and two of them were wounded during the shooting, maybe by our gunfire. Tillery rode closer to the barn.

"Everyone inside the tavern, the shed and the barn, you have one minute to get out and surrender before we torch them!"

"Wait - - -wait --- wait!"

The tavern owner and his family (wife, two sons and two daughters) came out of the tavern. Three men came out of the barn. One of them was the man who had deserted and warned the Tories.

Tillery had those three help the tavern owner and Vance dig a mass grave for our casualties. Vance didn't want to but Tillery made him put the men he led who were killed into the grave.

The militia wanted to hang the Tories and the deserter but instead we all took them to General Marion so he could question them.

I didn't hear Gerald Vance say anything else about being a natural born leader.

I've got to say that riding with General Marion and carrying messages from him opened my eyes to a lot of what was going on.

8

Camp Follower Gossip

July 11, 1781

Once again, I was sitting with Rob and his family of wife and mother-in-law. There were others and there were some changes. The widows who had been there couple of months earlier were now newly wedded women. There were also some new widows. I had brought two gallons of rum which was being poured into a variety of different cups.

I had just returned and Rob waited until I had a chance to sip my rum before he asked any questions. Before Rob had a chance to ask or say anything, one of the new widows spoke up.

"I reckon that we need more militia leaders like Elijah Clarke."

"What do you know about Elijah Clarke?"

The questioner was another camp follower I didn't remember seeing before. I sipped my rum figuring the women would make it easy for me to keep quiet.

Milly's Story about Elijah Clarke and war in Georgia

"First off, I know Elijah Clarke from down in Georgia. I reckon he's as fighting a man as ever came out of Georgia."

"What all has Elijah Clarke done?"

"First off, he come from North Carolina. He's married to my good friend, Hannah (she was a Harrington) and they been in Georgia for about eight or ten years now."

"First off, Elijah Clarke kind of sided with the King but that didn't last too long. Folks figure he was maybe pretending to side with the king to keep them off his back. Anyhow, he joined our militia and they made him a captain in a hurry. Folks knowed right off that Elijah Clarke was a fighting man. Folks said he done a right good job fighting the Cherokee in 76. He got wounded fighting the Cherokee too. The very next year, he led the militia against Creek raiders that were pestering us."

She stopped to breath but she wasn't ready to stop talking.

"First off, he done a real good job and they made him a colonel in the Georgia state militia. Right off, he got wounded again in Florida at the Battle of Alligator Bridge. Two year ago this past February, he charged his men at Kettle Creek and we won!"

"First off, that day, 600 Tories were camped on top of a hill above a bend of the creek. They were going to Augusta. They were led by an Irishman but I don't remember his name. It don't matter as he was killed that day anyhow."

"First off, all the Tories weren't from Georgia. About half were from North Carolina. I heard that the Irishman came down from New York. I don't remember where I heard that. I think I heard that

Jack More was leading the Tories from North Carolina."

"First off, those Tories were already being chased by a passel of our militia. They weren't doing much damage but they were chasing the Tories all the same. The Tories had already took Fort Independence and the fort at Broad Mouth Creek in South Carolina. Folks figured they would attack McGowan's Blockhouse in South Carolina but they didn't. Our militia at Cherokee Ford attacked the Tories but they didn't do much damage to them. In fact, the Tories took some of our men prisoner."

"First off, some of our spies found out that the Tories were supposed to get help from Augusta and that they had already turned back toward Savannah. Knowing this, Elijah Clarke helped by Andy Pickens were getting ready to attack the Tories at Kettle Creek. They had been pestering the Tory cavalry at Robert Carr's Fort near Beaverdam Creek but they figured to cut off the Tories and whip them."

"First off, Pickens took his men and attacked. He attacked right up that rocky hill above Kettle Creek while Elijah Clarke and a man named Dooly attacked the Tory camp across the creek on both sides. Pickens got in trouble because the men he sent to spy it out shot at the Tory sentries and told all the Tories they were being attacked."

I figured that some of the camp followers had heard this before but they were all paying attention like it was new news to them.

"First off, the Tories attacked back and were doing a pretty fair job until their leader got shot and killed deadern a lightning struck raccoon. After that, the Tories didn't know what to do and commenced running around like a bunch of chickens what had their heads chopped off. I heard that a bunch of Tories were killed and nigh two hundred took prisoner."

"First off, Georgia and most all of South Carolina was took by the British in 1780. That didn't stop Elijah Clarke. He took thirty men through the Cherokee land keep on fighting in South and

Elijah Clarke, Public Domain

North Carolina. I reckon that Elijah Clarke was nigh as good as the Swamp Fox - - - maybe even better. Clarke led his militia against the British and Tories, beating them up at Musgrove's Mill, Cedar Springs, Wofford's Iron Works, Augusta, Fishdam Ford, Long Cane, and Blackstocks. He might a not been at King's Mountain and Cowpens, but his fighting sure helped our side win those victories."

"First off, I know a lot of folks in Georgia who are good patriots. Why, I know a woman name of Nancy Hart and she aims to run all the British and Tories out of Georgia. I know for a fact that she captured nigh a dozen, killed at least that many and helped hang nine or ten. Folks claim she is a spy. I see you there a shaking your head like maybe I don't know what I'm talking about."

No one answered her.

"Well, I do. First off, her real name is Ann and folks just call her Nancy. She's taller than most men and can work with men all day long. Cherokee call her Wahatche and that means war woman. She knows herbs and barbs, she is a dead shot and she aint a woman you want to mess with."

"First off, while her husband is away fighting British and Tories. She works their farm when she aint off spying on the British. Folks say that she dressed like a man and would go in British and tory camps acting like a simple-minded man and get a sight of news. She gave a lot of news to patriots. She fought at the Battle of Kettle Creek and done a fine job. The British always suspected her but they wouldn't admit that a woman could do all that she did. They kept spying on her. One time, a Tory was spying through a break in her cabin's chinking. Nancy was making soap inside because it was a rainy day. She threw a dipper full of the lye and tallow mix through the hole in the chinking, scalding the Tory around his eye. Then she tied the Tory up and turned him over to the militia. I think she turned him over to Elijah Clarke."

The women were all paying attention now.

"First off, one time six British soldiers killed her last turkey. They made Nancy cook it for them saying they would hurt her children if she didn't. While she was cooking the turkey, she brought out a jug of homemade whiskey and had a sip. The British soldiers took the rest and got themselves drunk. Nancy sent her girl to get some water and warn some neighbors. While the British ate and drank the homemade whiskey, Nancy started sneaking their guns out through a window. She got caught and the British tried to grab her. Nancy shot one soldier with the musket he was getting ready to put out the window, then grabbed another musket and wounded another one. She grabbed a third musket and the rest of the British soldiers surrendered."

"First off, she had one British soldier tie up the others then she held a gun on him. When her neighbors got there, and saw what was going on, they sent someone for her husband. When he got there, they hung the British soldiers from a tree across from her cabin. I reckon that Nancy Hart is as tough as any man there is living."

Nancy Hart holding British soldier's prisoner   Public Domain

"Milly, you need to rest your mouth for a spell. I bet Nate wants to hear about how we took Augusta."

"First off, Janey, I . . . "

"I done told you Milly, Nate wants to hear about how we took Augusta. If he didn't he would have said so. Now you rest a spell and I'll let you talk more about Elijah Clarke later on. You tell me when to start, Nate."

"Start." It wasn't that I was over curious but I had heard all the 'first offs' that I wanted to hear for a while.

Janey's tale about the Siege of Augusta

"You probably know that the war started getting heated up in Georgia when the British captured Savannah back in November 1778. It got worse after we failed to capture Savannah with help from the French. It was rough but our militias didn't give up. Last April, Micajah Williamson took a bunch of militias and set up a kind of fort camp right outside of Augusta. The murdering Tory, Tom brown, was in charge of Fort Cornwallis there in Augusta. Micajah spread the word that he had a sight more men with him than he did and that kept the Tories at a distance. Augusta's main fort was Fort Cornwallis. Because the Tories thought we had a sight more men than we had, they didn't move on us."

I wondered where and how camp followers got so much information.

"General Andrew Pickens and Colonel Lee put Augusta under Siege in late May. General Pickens had around 400 men set up between Augusta and Ninety-Six, to stop the British and Tories at Ninety-Six from sending help to Tom Brown at Augusta. Before the siege began, Micajah Williamson was joined by Elijah Clarke and around a hundred men. This was enough to stop any more supplies from reaching Tom Brown and his murdering Tories."

Everyone was listening. Someone poured me another dram of rum that I appreciated.

"General Greene had told Colonel Lee to try to capture of Ninety-Six, but when Lee got close to Ninety-Six, he soon found out that Ninety-Six was too forted up for Lee to make a dent in it. He sent word to General Greene and General Greene told him to go help General Pickens at Augusta. Now even before they started the siege, a day or two before. Elijah Clarke and Light Horse Harry attacked a stockade that was the house of a British Indian agent by the name of George Galphin. There were British soldiers and a bunch of Tory militia there. It was over pretty quick and the Tories gave up and surrendered after half a dozen of them were killed and bunch wounded. We lost one dead of the heat and some wounded. Over 125 British soldiers and Tory militia surrendered. The biggest help that winning the fight was to us was the provisions, for the British and the supplies and military equipment they had aimed to give to the Indians to use against us."

"Very good, Janey, very good! Now let me tell Nate about Fort Grierson!"

"Go ahead, Lizzie, tell him!"

By now the two jugs of rum I'd brought were gone and every one was feeling pretty warmed up. Some other whiskey had been brought from somewhere and all the camp followers seemed relaxed.

Lizzie's Tale about Fort Grierson

"So, Fort Grierson was about half a mile from Fort Cornwallis. It fort was defended by about 80 or 90 men under Colonel Grierson. Right after Pickens and Lee commenced the siege, within a day or two, some our militias commenced circling around the fort to keep Grierson from giving any help to Fort Cornwallis. The murdering Tory, tom Brown, caught on to this pretty quick and fetched some of his men from Fort Cornwallis to give Colonel Grierson some help. All his ideas of rescuing Grierson run off pretty quick as soon as he saw that old Light Horse Harry was ready for him. Brown got him and his men back in Fort Cornwallis just as quick as he could. He shot at Lee's force with some cannon but didn't do any damage.

So, Elijah Clarke's men had been bad wronged by Tom Brown and his bunch. Brown had had murdered innocents people and abused helpless women and Elijah's men were out for blood. When Grierson figured that he was trapped where he was at, he and all his men tried to get away by retreating down the riverbank. They didn't get far before Elijah Clarke's men caught them. That's right, they caught Grierson and his whole company. They caught them all! Then Elijah's men, remembering all the murders and wrong that Tom Brown and his men had done, took their revenge on Brown by giving no quarter and killing Grierson and all his men."

I noticed that none of the camp followers seemed put out at the killing of Grierson's and his men. Lizzie went on with her story.

"So, there was about 300 Tory militia and 200 slaves with Tom Brown inside Fort Cornwallis. It was a strong fort and was well made. Out men were having a devil of a time figuring out how to attack it, since they only had one cannon, when old Light Horse Harry came up with an idea. He said that they should build a tower that would let them shoot right down inside the fort. He said they had done something like that at the Siege of Fort Watson and it had worked real good. So, they commenced building a tower. While they were building the tower, Brown sent men out of the fort to attack our men but Lee's men fought them off each time. I hear that our men did a good job of fighting there.

"So, it took a few days but they built a tower over thirty feet high. I hear that our men were able to put their one cannon on top of the tower. Our men commenced shooting right down into the fort. Our men killed a sight of the Tories and that night, Brown and all his men left the fort and attacked our men. It didn't do him nary bit of good thought. Our men run them back inside the fort like you'd run a puppy out of a kitchen with a switch."

Some of the camp followers laughed and clapped at Lizzie's description. This encouraged her to go on.

"So, Brown sent out one of his men who pretended to be a deserter. He aimed for the man to get to the tower and set it on fire. He told Colonel Lee that he could put the cannon on top of the tower and shoot the cannon down into the fort at the fort's magazine. He almost had Colonel Lee convinced but old Light Horse Harry got suspicious and put him under guard. Our cannon on top of the tower kept right on being shot at the inside of the fort. The cannon destroyed the barracks and destroyed their cannon mounts. We were planning an attack on the fort when the last house near the fort blew up. Brown had sent men to set charges in the house because he figured we would fill it with our men but it blew up before we put any men in the building.

So, the next morning, General Pickens and Colonel Lee sent in a surrender demand. Brown turned it down saying he couldn't surrender on the King's birthday. Pickens agreed to wait one day. The next day, down. In deference to the fact that it was the King's birthday, the attack was delayed one day. The next day, Brown offered to talk about surrender."

"Lizzie, did they kill Brown?"

"No, they had him surrender to Continental Soldiers because they were afraid Brown would get just what Grierson got. He deserved that kind of treatment too."

I wondered if General Greene knew how much camp followers knew about what was going on. Probably not, I would never have guessed it before Rob and Ann wed and she and her mother decided to travel with him. No, I don't know how they get all the news. The only thing I can come up with is that gossip must get to women faster than any other force in the country.

I was considering the possible answers when Rob nudged me to get my attention.

"Nate, seeing that you been with General Marion, is he as good a spy as some folks say?"

I sipped enough of the rum and water to start my head a buzzing like a half-filled hornet's nest before I answered. I didn't want to short change General Marion when I told about him.

The Swamp Fox as a Spy

"He's better. Militia that's led right has done a lot of good things in South Carolina. Marion has led his right. They've attacked British patrols and outposts. They've put the fear of God into the Tories. They've captured supplies on both land and on the Pee Dee, Santee and Congaree Rivers. They collected cattle, salt, and provisions for militia use and to stop them from being taken by the British. Marion got news for both General Horatio Gates and General Nathanael Greene - - - they might not have made the best use of the news but he got them the news. Maybe the best thing he has to offer is he's better able to fight like Indians in the woods and swamps. Some of us might not know much about lining up on as field for a pitched battle but we can dern sure pester their supply shipments and patrols to there and back. Trained militia can fight almost as good as battle tested veterans - - - if the militia have good leadership."

"How many men does he have? We hear that they come and go when they want to go."

"They come and go. While the militia stay home, they discourage Tories from joining the British. While at home, they get supplies for the Continental army. They still pester the British every way they can. You might say the militia at home are foxes in the British chicken pen."

"Nate, how does Marion rate as a leader?"

"General Marion is one of the best militia leaders. He's got a sight more victories than losses. He controls a large area between the Pee Dee and Santee Rivers. Even though General Gates got his tail whipped at Camden. Marion was smart about recruiting, training and leading militia. He does much more than raise men, train them, and lead them in battle. He's served as a spy for General Greene ever since Green relieved Gates of command of the Southern Army."

"Nate, I didn't know that!"

"That's right Rob. Green told Marion to get him news about British troop movements, troop strength, deaths from combat and disease, and anything that might affect their operations. So, added to his duties of raising, training, and leading a brigade of farmers, planters, tradesmen, and blacksmiths, Marion looked for news that would help Greene's army. This wasn't easy at first because Marion has no training in getting news and making sure it's real. He has no training in separating fact from rumor. He received no funds to pay for information or spying - - - but he has done a dern good job. As scarce as paper is, Marion sends several letters to Greene each week with news about British strength and movements. I understand that his reports got better and better. He learned how to report facts and ignore rumors. He learned that if he sent a rumor, that he had to say it was a rumor. He hardly ever sent rumors of victories or defeats that he couldn't prove. He learned to pay a lot of attention to troop movements so that Greene would know in advance if he was about to be hit by a much bigger force than he had to fight back."

"Nate, I didn't know all that either."

"Few knew it. These reports were real important before and after General Morgan whipped Tarleton at the Cowpens. This was important because Greene's force was too small to fight a large British force until he gathered Morgan's force and Huger's force with his army. Both Greene's force and Morgan's force would have been in a trick if they had to face the main part of Cornwallis's army. They were spared this problem because Marion sent good and true news about the moving of the British as they waded through rain and mud toward Winnsboro. Other militia officers sent news but Marion sent the news about Leslie's march to Greene. He was also the first militia leader to learn that Leslie's troops had got in South Carolina. He was also the first militia commander to find out that British soldiers had left Charleston when they started their mud slogging march toward Cornwallis. Marion's reports let Greene escape from Cornwallis when the British invaded North Carolina after Leslie's troops joined him."

"What about after the Battle of the Cowpens, Nate?"

"Greene's army and Morgan's detachment were tickled to death by Morgan's victory at the Cowpens but they were still too small to handle Cornwallis' army. Greene retreated all the way to the Dan River, crossing it into Virginia taking all the boats to the Virginia side of the river. The retreat was through mud, rain, sleet and cold winds. Greene got a lot of reinforcements after he got to Virginia. He also got enough supplies to continue. Cornwallis had burned all the supplies his army couldn't carry and had marched away from his line of supply and reinforcement. With more men and more supplies, Greene went looking for a fight. After pestering the British with his newly formed light corps, he took his army to the region around Guilford Courthouse and prepared to fight. Cornwallis attacked. The battle was real bloody and real desperate. Cornwallis claimed victory but his army lost over a fourth of its men and officers."

"We remember the Battle of Guilford Courthouse, Nate. Folks say we lost."

"The British lost 29 officers killed or wounded. A general was seriously wounded and two regimental commanders died from their wounds. Greene's losses weren't as bad. The biggest loss was about 800 North Carolina militia who left the battlefield and went home. Of course, since they left, Greene didn't have to worry about wasting supplies on them. Marion wasn't at Guilford courthouse but the news he kept sending Greene allowed Greene to avoid a battle until he was ready. Instead of having to fight a larger British army before he was ready, he was able to cripple Cornwallis's army at Guilford Courthouse. Rather than return to South Carolina, Cornwallis retreated into Virginia to unite his army with a strong well supplied detachment commanded by Major-General William Phillips."

I stopped while one of the women, I recognized her as one of the new widows, poured first rum, then water into my cup. I took a drink, then a few sips before I went on with the tale.

"After trailing Cornwallis for a while, Greene turned south and moved his army toward Camden. After getting close to Marion, Greene made sure to make good use of him. He was already planning on how to get rid of British posts. He started by planning to stop the British supplies from getting to the British posts. Then Greene moved parts of his army to the areas controlled by Marion and Sumter This means that Marion and Sumter find themselves fighting in the front lines. They've had a spell of partisan fighting now. Greene has made sure he cooperated with Marion and Sumter. He sent Light Horse Harry Lee and a detachment of dragoons and mounted infantry to help Marion. Together they used information Marion's men gathered to defeat British outposts along the Congaree and Wateree Rivers. The outposts were captured one by one as Marion and Lee carried out a series of successful siege operations. A small British post, called Fort Watson, was the first to fall. Before the end of April, Marion was able to send to Greene the agreeable intelligence that the fort had been captured, together with its entire garrison with all their arms and ammunition. A real interesting thing about the siege of Fort Watson was the use of a Maham Tower. Towers like it had been used in the siege of Medieval castles and cities, but Major Hezekiah Maham of Marion's brigade adapted them for siege operations in South Carolina. This is where Colonel Lee got the idea for a tower at the Augusta siege. The first of his towers was a structure built of crossed logs with a rifle platform at the top. During the course of the campaign, such towers were made larger and stronger until they could support the weight of field pieces as well as that of several sharpshooters. While Lee and Marion were occupied with siege operations, Greene was unable to march to help them because he was held in check by the garrison of Camden, commanded by Francis, Lord Rawdon. Because of the way that Lee and Marion tore up his supply situation by pestering his supply lines, Rawdon was forced to either leave Camden or risk starving. Before Rawdon lit out, however, Greene was asking Marion for news about British defenses in South

Carolina. When Rawdon's British infantry retreated, Marion gave Greene real information as it moved to the south side of the Santee River. Of course, then Greene led his army west to besiege the fort at Ninety-Six. He hoped to capture it before Lord Rawdon could march to its relief, but the garrison resisted stubbornly and the siege dragged on through several weeks of May and June."

I figured that much talking deserved another drink so I took one from my cup. One of the widows made sure my cup was taken care of and I wondered if I should remind them that I had a wife and family. Instead, I kept on with my tale telling.

"While all this was happening, more battalions of British infantry arrived at Charlestown from England. Rawdon picked the best troops from among the new soldiers and led them on forced marches through hot, muggy weather to save Ninety-Six. When the British army marched out of Charleston, Marion sent the bad news to Greene. And as the redcoats hurried westward, first Marion and then Sumter sent forward news of their advance. This is how come Greene to know that a relief column was on its way to mess up his siege operations. Looking back, Greene shouldn't have tried to take the fort by storming it. We got beat back and took heavy losses. Of course, the British had to leave Ninety-six and Greene's Continentals occupied Ninety-Six after they left. Marion's capture of Fort Watson and other British posts in the valleys of the Congaree and Wateree had cut the supply lines between Ninety-Six and the British bases in the low country."

"Nate, is he still doing this?"

"When the two armies reached the lowlands, Marion made himself real useful to General Greene. He keeps on sending news to Greene and he has to keep on skirmishing with the British. When he can find time, he raises men, trains them, and finds cattle and provisions for the American army. Maybe one of the most important his jobs this summer is finding food and fodder for Greene's troops and keeping the British from getting them. Driving cattle and carrying off supplies of corn, rice, and salt may not be heroic work.

But it has to be done. Marion' keeps his men riding widely through the country south of the Santee on their foraging missions. Marion figures this will keep the British in Charlestown and keep them from stealing food from the farmers. He also had his men drive all the cattle they could find to the north side of the Santee to keep them farther from the British. Busy as Marion is with skirmishing, foraging, and raising men, Marion keeps on getting news to General Greene."

I picked up a jug and shook it. It didn't have much but I poured it into Rob's cup. He started to sip it but his mother-in-law made sure it was watered down first.

"Now Rob, tell me what happened at Ninety-Six."

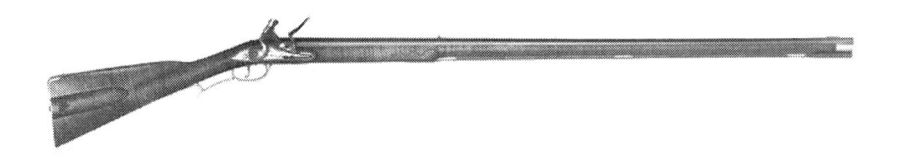

9

Attack on Ninety-Six

Ninety Six was established in western South Carolina maybe 60 or 80 years before. Folks used to call it Jews Land on account of several rich Jewish families back in London had bought a sight of land there, over 200,000 acres, aiming to help some poor Jewish families from London settle there.

Ninety-Six was heard of a lot during the Cherokee War of 1758 through 1761. Militia and soldiers were kept there to defend western settlements and farms. Ninety-Six was also a jumping off place for campaigns against the Cherokee.

When South Carolina established the Ninety-Six District in 1769, Ninety-Six was made capital of the district. There are a lot of tales told about how Ninety-Six got its name. I can't say for sure, but the tale that it is ninety-six miles from a Cherokee town called Keowe sounds as good as any.

Ninety-Six has seen a lot of fighting in this war too. The first land battle south of New England was fought there in 1775. On August 1, 1775, militia led by Major Andy Williamson were ambushed by Cherokee and Tories in the Battle of Twelve Mile Creek. The British and Tories had encouraged over 4,000 Cherokee to attack Patriots all the way from the settlements on the Watauga to south central South Carolina.

In 1780, after they captured Charlestown, the British fortified Ninety-Six with a star fort. That might have been enough for some but they weren't finished. In fact, they acted like fortifying fools. They stole a bunch of slaves and used their labor to dig a ditch, eight feet deep, around the whole fort. They took the dirt they dug up and used to strengthen the walls. Short of having a lot of cannon, I wasn't sure the fort could have been taken as long as it had outside support.

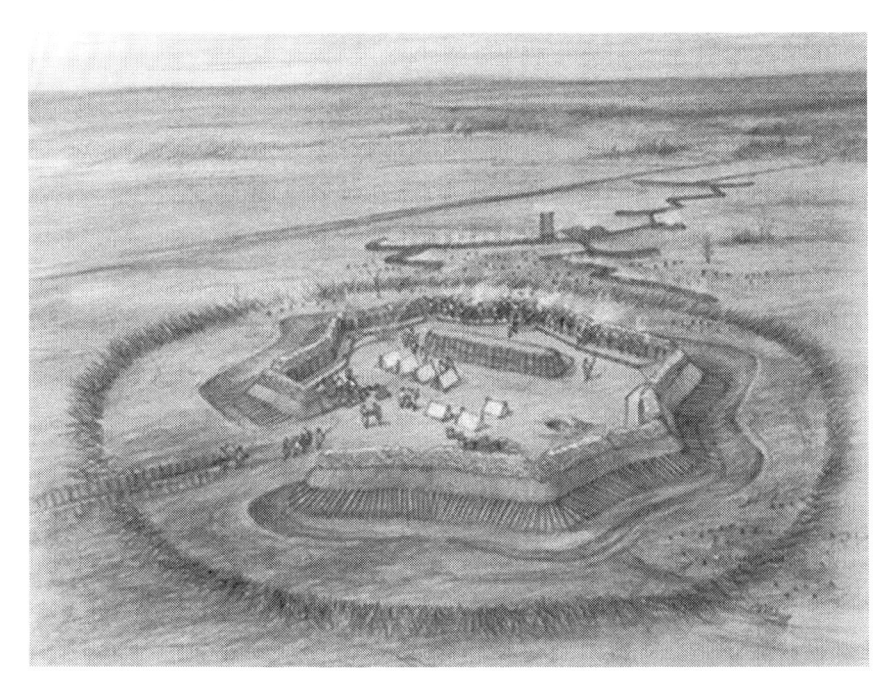

We had captured a lot of couriers carrying the message to Cruger at Ninety-Six telling him to abandon the fort and join Brown at Augusta. It might have been better for us if he had received one of the messages. It's hard to tell.

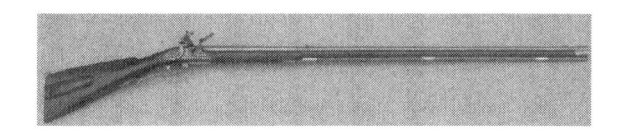

Rob's Tale about the Battle of Ninety-Six

General Greene got us to Ninety-Six on, I think on May twenty-first or twenty-second. It was raining and I guess we were all soaked to the skin. This might a been the same storm you told us about Nate. General Greene and that officer from Poland[5] rode around Ninety-Six. I reckon that was the first time that Greene really got a hint of how strong the fort was. I heard that General Greene was real surprised at how strong the fort was. The next morning, General Greene sent a message to Lafayette saying that Ninety-Six might be too strong for him to take.

As it turned out, there wasn't a single British regular at Ninety-Six. Every man inside Ninety-six was an American Tory. The Tories included 150 men of Cruger's Second Battalion of New York Volunteers, over 200 veterans from the New Jersey Volunteers, and about 200 Tory militia recruited nearby under the command of General Robert Cunningham, that dern South Carolina tory. There were also about a hundred Tory citizens and a big labor battalion of slaves they had stolen.

Now, we were a pretty strong force ourselves. We had over 400 experienced and battle-tested Continentals from

---

[5] Count Thaddeus Kosciusko

Maryland and Delaware, over 400 Virginia militia, over 60 North Carolina militia, and around 60 men in Captain Robert Kirkwood's scout company from Delaware. After the British and Tories at Augusta gave up, we got the militia under Colonel Lee and General Pickens to help us out.

General Greene didn't even bother to ask Cruger to surrender. He had men commence right off digging parallel approaches that would get us closer to the Star Redoubt so we could set gunpowder charges to blow up the defenses. We were digging the parallels ab out seventy-five yards from the fort. This turned out to be a mistake.

Cruger put three or four cannon on top of the bunkers and loaded them up with grapeshot and something called canister and commenced shooting at the men digging the parallels. After a few cannon shots, Cruger sent a couple dozen men to attack the men digging the ditch. Our men were killed with bayonets and all the tools stolen by some slaves who were with the British attack. I think the British lost one man killed, the leader of the attack.

Greene General Greene pulled us back to about four hundred yards *to* a safer distance. He ordered the digging of parallels to begin there. He ordered cannon fire and rifle fire from log defenses to protect the diggers. This was safer but the digging was tiring. We dug day and night to finish the job. I don't know if the officer from Poland got any sleep at all. It seemed like he was always watching the digging. We got closer but it was slow going.

What we didn't know was how scarce rations were getting inside Ninety-Six. If we had known, we could have just tried to starve them out. We didn't know so we kept right on digging. By early June, we finished the second parallel and were between fifty and sixty yards of the fort.

General Greene pushed us hard to finish the third parallel into the Star Fort. We were doing a good job but we began getting fire from the Tory riflemen. Greene had some men build a Maham tower about thirty yards from the fort's ditch and close to the line of the third parallel. Our snipers, climbed up the log tower and opened up on the Tory riflemen. Our shooters ran off the Tory shooters and forced them down below the parapet. Not a Tory would show his head on the wall without getting it shot off.

Having the advantage, General Greene called for Cruger to surrender. He sent Colonel Otho Williams of the First Maryland to warn Cruger that the British army was too far away to help him and that a bunch of British forts like Fort Watson and Fort Motte had been forced to surrender. Through Otho Williams, General Greene demanded immediate and unconditional surrender. He further warned Cruger against further resistance.

Cruger rejected the surrender demand.

The Maham tower was causing Cruger a lot of problems. To solve the problem of the tower, Cruger raised the Star Fort bunkers three feet higher with sandbags and leaving holes for his Tory riflemen to shoot through. This didn't solve all the problems and Cruger tried to destroy the tower by firing heated cannon balls into the tower. Since the tower logs were green and the shooters didn't have a proper way to heat the cannon balls, the tower didn't catch fire.

General Greene didn't stop at digging the parallels. He did a lot of things to pester the Tories inside the fort into surrendering. He had soldiers use bows and arrows to try to set the roofs inside the fort on fire. It didn't work. Cruger had his men tear off the roofs so the arrows wouldn't set them on fire. If Cruger hadn't had the roof's torn off, the wooden shingles would have been set afire and the fire could have spread. Tearing off the shingles left the Tory soldiers open to the weather but it kept the buildings from being burned. Greene had heard that this very thing had worked at Fort Motte. Greene had his soldiers dip arrows into pitch, light the

Rise & Fight

arrows and fire them into the fort. Cruger's ordering his men to take off the roofs stopped the threat from the fire arrows.

After the attack on Augusta, Light Horse Harry and his legion came up to Ninety-Six. Greene gave Lee the job of attacking Fort Holmes on the side of the village across from the Star. Lee commenced digging parallel ditches toward the smaller fort and made good progress. Every night, soldiers from Fort Holmes charged out of the fort to try to drive off Lee's Legion and protect their water supply. Every night, there was fierce and bloody fighting with both sides losing men. In four or five days, Lee was in a position to shoot into both Fort Holmes and the stream the fort got their water from. When he was in that position, it cut the men in Fort Holmes off from their drinking water and it being June, it caused them a lot of suffering. We found out later that the British inside Fort Holmes began digging a well inside the fort but they didn't find any water. The only water the Tories in the fort got for about a week was the little bit that naked slaves brought in at night. Those slaves risked their lives by slipping down into the ravine to get a bucket of water and take it back to the fort. Sometimes I think that if we'd cut off their water earlier, we could have forced the forts to surrender.

Lee told Greene a plan to burn the fort and I guess Greene told him to go ahead and Lee made another try at burning the stockade. On a dark and cloudy day, a sergeant and nine men toting bundles of dry grass and wood covered with pitch sneaked into the enemy's ditch, but before they could set them afire, they were seen by a sentry who sounded the alarm. Cruger sent soldiers into the ditch and the sergeant was killed along with five of his men. The other four soldiers escaped to our lines.

While all this was a going on, General Greene had pushed the third ditch to within ten feet or so the British defenses. On about June 10 or 11, the engineer from Poland Kosciusko figured that the ditch we were digging would reach the ditch around the star fort in a day or two. Greene planned to tunnel under the Star Fort's outer fortifications and set gunpowder to made a path for us to assault through the bunkers.

I know for a fact that General Greene sent a message to General Pickens asking for gunpowder.[6] It might a worked but Greene had to stop the siege before we could dig our way inside the fort.

Greene was afraid that British reinforcements from Charlestown would come to rescue Ninety-Six before Cruger surrendered. He was right to worry because Colonel Rawdon was getting a relief party together. Rawdon was but thanks to General Marion sending the news to Greene, he knew how long he had before the British arrived to relieve Cruger.

Like you told us a while ago, Nate, General Greene had set up a great spying system in South Carolina to keep him told about what the British were doing. Like you told us a while ago, Nate, General Marion was maybe the best man Greene has to find out what the British are doing and getting word to General Greene. The word was that General Greene had told General Marion that "Spies are the Eyes of an Army, and without them a General is always groping in the dark ... It is of highest Importance that I get the earliest information about any reinforcements which may arrive at Charlestown. ... " Not only have I got that on good authority, I got it from the man who carried the

---

[6] *We are in immediate want of a few barrels of powder to compleat the reduction of this place. We shall be in the ditch of the enemies works by tomorrow night or next morning; and the powder is wanting to blow up the works. I beg you will send the powder the moment this reaches you.*

message to General Marion.

Greene instructed Marion to "fix some Plan for procuring such Information and for conveying it to me with all possible dispatch."

During the siege of Ninety-Six, General Greene's spy system proved to be worth all the time and trouble he and others had put into it. When three ships full of Irish regulars arrived in Charlestown in early June to reinforce Colonel Rawdon, word was relayed to General Greene in just four or five days. When Colonel Rawdon marched to relieve the Ninety-Six, Greene knew it within three days.

News that Colonel Rawdon was coming with over two thousand men made it clear to General Greene that he had to either capture the fort quick or back off the job.

Greene tried to delay Rawdon's movement into the interior. He told General Thomas Sumter, to "collect all the force you can and skirmish with the enemy all the way they advance, removing out of their way all the cattle and means of transportation and subsistence. It is my wish to have the enemy galled as much as possible in penetrating the country."

Greene's plan didn't work. In fact, it probably barely pestered Rawdon. Instead of following the shortest way to Ninety-Six, Rawdon traveled in a longer route which was a thirteen-day march from Charlestown, but allowed Rawdon to completely by-pass Sumter and avoid the cavalry units under Colonel Andrew Pickens and Colonel William Washington who General Greene sent out to catch him.

From Charleston, the British tried to get word to Cruger that help for him was on the way. A farmer was riding along our lines. Nobody paid any attention to him because curious folks wandered in and out of the battle lines when the fighting was eased off. They were a common sight. In front of the stockade gate, the farmer hollered and, spurred his horse into the fort while thirty or so of our men shot at him. He passed on the news to Cruger that Rawdon was coming and was near the Little Saluda River. Any thoughts Cruger and his men had of surrendering were done away with by the news. Greene heard about Colonel Rawdon's position from his spies on the same day.

Siege tactics didn't break through the defenses at Ninety-Six. General Greene ordered an assault. I gather he wasn't real happy about the idea but Greene thought that while the attack had little chance of success, but that we had to try before Rawdon got there.

In spite thinking there was little chance of success, Greene started the final attack with a cannon barrage at noon on June 18. We attacked both forts, Holmes' Fort and the Star. The fighting was bloody and short. Colonel Lee's Legionnaires, helped by Captain Kirkwood's Delaware scouts, drove the British from the Fort Holmes, but the main assault on the Star didn't work.

We failed but it wasn't for lack of trying. Attacking under cannon fire, the American attack led by two lieutenants entered the ditch surrounding the Star Fort. They charged into heavy musket fire from the enemy. Our men threw grappling hooks and began tearing down the sandbag defense so that we could climb over the bunkers and into the Star Fort. Heavy artillery and rifle fire from the tower covered the attack. The British sent out two parties of thirty men each to drive off our advance party in the ditch. It was a vicious attack from two sides. We lost two-thirds of our attackers. About forty men, were killed or wounded and our attack was broken. After almost an hour, Greene ordered the attack called off.

After the attack was ended, Greene offered to swap prisoners with the British and Cruger said yes. Greene also asked an exchange of burial details to bury the dead of both armies that fell between the lines and within the trenches. I think that only our dead were outside the British defenses and Cruger ordered our dead carried out so we could bury them.

On June 19, Greene stopped the siege. He knew we could be bad hurt if we tried to fight the two thousand regulars with Rawdon while we were still fighting Cruger and his Tories. We retreated east, to the other side of Bush River. On June 21, after a forced march Rawdon's army reached Ninety-Six. He sent a bunch to chase us, but they didn't come close because we had a two-day's march lead and the British too wore out from their march from Charlestown to get close.

Aint it something though, if Green had known Rawdon wanted Cruger to abandon Ninety-Six and Cruger had known Rawdon wanted him to go to Augusta, I wonder what would have happened.

John Harris Cruger, Black and white version of a color painting by Robert W. Wilson. Used with the artist's permission.

10

Rising

    I wasn't as put out about General Greene having to retreat from Ninety-Six as some others. I'd spent so much time riding, carrying messages and spying that I had a better idea of what was going on all over South Carolina than most men in the army and militia had. While the Swamp Fox and Light Horse Harry were capturing Fort Watson and Fort Motte, General Sumter had attacked and captured the British posts at Orangeburg and Granby. I figured that Colonel Rawdon was afraid that all the different American forces would hit Camden at once that caused him to abandon and destroy that British post. That and the fact that the posts that were supposed to provide safety for supplies going to Camden and Ninety-Six had been captured.

    While Greene was attacking Ninety-Six, Colonel Brown at Augusta couldn't send help because Pickens, later helped by Light Horse Harry, was attacking Augusta. General Sumter was raiding down the country pestering the British and trying to stop the British from stealing cattle from the people. Sumter was in a hurry to unite all the South Carolina forces and attack Rawdon. General Greene did not think much of that idea as

I guess he figured that going slow and protecting the army was the better choice. Marion and Sumter tried to slow down Rawdon while Greene was trying to take Ninety-Six.

What it all came down to was that there was fighting going on all over South Carolina and Georgia, not just at Ninety-Six. We were not just pestering the British, in a lot of places we were beating them.

While Greene was attacking Ninety-Six, the British in Charlestown were making plans for ravaging the country on the south side of the Santee River. They aimed to steal everything they could and destroy all the Patriot property that they could. The Tories at Charlestown had been formed into a regiment under Colonel Ball and were itching to do all the stealing and destroying that they could do. But Marion was ready. I had joined him and with his other spies, found out everything that was going on in Charlestown. The Swamp Fox didn't have enough men to fight the whole British army in Charlestown. Instead, he took all the stock, cattle and all the provisions, that he could find across the Santee to safe places. This saved the stock and for the American army and kept them from the British.

Marion was as ready to fight the British as Sumter. He sent me to Greene at Ninety-Six asking for help covering more country. Greene sent Colonel Will Washington to help General Marion. pressing dispatches to Greene for assistance in covering the country. Like I said, Sumter and Marion were supposed to be doing enough to keep Rawdon away from Greene and they were doing a pretty good job until a British fleet got to Charlestown with three regiments of reinforcements from Ireland made it possible for Rawdon to ignore any actions Sumter and Marion might take. To Marion's credit, he sent word to Greene through Sumter on the same day the reinforcements arrived.

Now, Rawdon has already abandoned Ninety-six and was back in Charlestown. From that day forward, keeping Charlestown became Rawdon's main job. With South Carolina militia led by the likes of Marion and Sumter, Rawdon could not control the state. The British line of forts going all the way out to Ninety-Six and Augusta were gone. The line of Forts from Orangeburg to Ninety-Six was gone.

When the British abandoned Ninety-Six and lost the line of forts, the Tories had two choices; either change sides or abandon their property and flee to Charlestown. Within a year, the Tories had gone from holding aces to being without cards. The Tories who had taken advantage of the British army to attack Patriots and steal or destroy their property were suddenly without protection.

When Greene was told that Rawdon was taking all his forces that remained to Charlestown, he turned his army and followed Rawdon. It was at Ancrum's ferry on the Congaree that General Greene, traveling ahead of his army, joined General Marion with his four hundred militia and Colonel Washington with his two corps of cavalry.

A good thing about Greene coming ahead for me was that Rob was one of his escorts. Now, don't get me wrong, Rob still had some aging to do but he had bettered himself a right smart. Right then, he was having some trouble understanding his bride, Ann.

"Nate, I just don't understand her. We can go to sleep at night with her as lovey-dovey as can be - - - as warm and comforting as the best brandy. I wake up the next morning and not only aint I doing not anything right - - - I find out that I aint never done nothing right. It's like going to sleep with the finest brandy and waking up with green persimmon juice."

"Rob, how long has Ann been carrying a child?"

"I don't know. What's that got to do with it?"

"Well, Ann's probably about three or four months along and it has a lot to do with it. When a woman is with child, carrying a baby inside her, she is apt to be crazy part of the time. Not bad crazy - - - just crazy enough to act like she is real bad crazy. Women can't help it and we just got to learn how to put up with it."

"Are you sure?"

"I'm sure. You just need to remember not to get mad at her. Don't even argue with her. Just tell her that she's beautiful and that you love her. Tell her you can't get along without her."

"Will that take care of all the problem?"

"Hell no! She's a woman and she's with child. I told you that a woman with child is apt to act crazy."

Greene and Marion moved their troops down the Orangeburg road and were able to pass Lord Rawdon. They were able, shortly, to pass Colonel Rawdon's force. Greene kept Washington's cavalry and sent Marion with his mounted militia to capture a valuable convoy meant for the relief of Rawdon's army. Marion didn't reach the convoy because the convoy took a different road. Two days later, Rawdon and the convoy met at Orangeburg. Rawdon's soldiers were too tired to continue.

There were signs that the three regiments from Ireland would quit if ordered to continue. Major Carter mentioned to us that South Carolina summers were hotter than the British soldiers were used to living in.

As wore out as the British were, there defenses were too strong for Greene to attack with the men he had. Rawdon has his three regiments, Cruger with thirteen hundred men and the supply convoy with a hundred fifty men.

Greene had been pushing the idea that all the militia and state forces in South Carolina should unite and make major moves against the British. Rob was all in favor of this but I had my doubts.

"Nate, don't it make sense that the sooner that we whip the British, the sooner this war is over and we can get back home and our families?"

"Rob, we talked a lot about the Battle of King's Mountain and how we whipped Ferguson and either killed or captured all of his army. Do you know how the army that beat him was led and commanded?"

"Well, no."

"I do. I was there and I saw it. Might be that the best man to have led it was Ike Shelby. He knew that he couldn't because the other colonels were senior to him. He and the other colonels knew that the senior colonel was an older man and was not up to the job any longer. All the colonels were North Carolina colonels and they all knew that the man who was put in charge might be put higher than the rest after the campaign was successful."

"So, what'd they do?"

"Ike Shelby went to Colonel Will Campbell of the Virginia militia and told him that he should be in charge. Will Campbell had to be talked into it but it was agreed that all the colonels would meet each day after supper and decide what to do."

"So, how'd that go?"

"How'd it go! You know how it went! We whipped Ferguson like he was a stolen donkey! No North Carolina colonel had to worry about their honor and they got the job done."

"Okay?"

"Tell me Rob, do you think that General Sumter would serve under anyone else? When Greene sent for him to meet him at Camden, did Sumter come? No! He didn't! When Sumter was attacked by Tarleton with a fourth of the men Sumter had with him, was Sumter ready? No! Sumter and his men were routed! Do the other generals and colonels in the South Carolina Militia and the South Carolina State force have confidence in General Sumter?"

"I don't know?"

"I don't think so!"

"What do you think will happen?"

"I think that General Marion will give it a chance and that other leaders will do it because they respect General Marion. They won't do it because of any respect for Sumter."

It happened like I thought it would. Greene pushed the idea and Marion said he would give it a try. I hoped that it would work but I didn't have high hopes.

General Greene's encouraging the South Carolina militias and state troops to join together in attacking the British was finally given a try. I reckon that all or most of them were ready to fight under General Greene but many of them weren't real tickled by the idea of fighting under General Sumter's command. That's because the most senior brigadier general of South Carolina forces was Thomas Sumter. A lot of the other officers in the state figured that Sumter had such a bad case of the big head that they, and there were a lot of them, avoided him. Since the fall of Charlestown, a bunch of officers including some regiment leaders had refused to ever follow Sumter again.

I asked Rob if he and any idea how the camp followers knew so much about what was going on in the Carolinas and Georgia but he said he didn't know. We both agreed that gossip was faster than anything we had ever seen.

Gossip had to be fast to keep up with us as long as we had men like General Marion and Colonel Wade Hampton. Men like them made things happen.

Colonel Wade Hampton was another fighting South Carolinian. When General Sumter told him to ride towards Biggin Creek Bridge and aggravate any British posts in the area, he attacked 15-Mile House[7] with such fierceness that the British surrendered before any were killed. The success continued at 10-Mile House where the British surrendered, preferring being prisoners to risking death.

Colonel Hampton continued his job of aggravating the British by capturing Goose Creek Bridge with little opposition from the South Carolina Tories at the bridge. The Tories that weren't taken prisoner retreated to the Quarter House. Hampton and his men continued the attack, skirmishing with the Tories and attacking the Quarter House. Again, the garrison at the Quarter House surrendered except for a man who tried to escape. He was killed.

The next morning, he stopped at a farm and the woman told him that two boats were up the river a little piece with British soldiers and they were in the cornfield stealing roasting corn and beans.

Hampton took his patrol to the river bank. He had half of his men dismount and board the boats. There was only one British soldier on one of the two boats. He aimed his musket at them but the prime was wet and he couldn't shoot. Hampton's men shot him before he could replace the priming. Hampton's men searched the corn fields nearby and took thirty prisoners. Hampton paroled the British soldiers and burned the two boats. He found that the boats were loaded with indigo. Hampton and his men stayed for two hours eating the enemy's food and drinking their wine and rum. They only left when they were warned that British dragoons were coming. They went up the Ashley River and found a quiet spot to

---

[7] Called 15 Mile House because it was 15 miles from Charlestown

rest. Every man sat and held his horse until morning.

Hampton's week long aggravation of the British put the whole city of Charlestown in confusion. I reckon that the British command was so messed up they didn't know whether to go to a tavern or to a privy.

General Marion and some others were in a hurry to whip the British so they decided that General Greene's idea was worth trying. Like I said, I had some hopes that we might make it work and was glad to be part of the whole shebang. We were given the assignment of stopping British led by a Colonel Coates from returning to Charlestown from the area around Orangeburg with a huge amount of supplies.

The command was given to Sumter. Under Sumter were Marion, Lee, the Hamptons, Taylor, Horry, Maham, and others been actively aggravating and fighting the British for a long time. The command had all the State troops, Lee's legion, and a cannon. Our job was to strike at the British and distract Rawdon's attention from the Congaree, where he was trying to build up his force.

Sumter's force was broken into separate details. Colonel Lee pressed on to Dorchester, which surrendered. Colonel Wade Hampton aggravated the British in Charlestown, capturing the guard and patrol at the Quarter House while spreading terror through the city. Sumter and Marion then rode against the British at Biggin, held by Colonel Coates of the British army. Coates led a garrison of five hundred infantry, one hundred and fifty horse, and one cannon. The post at Biggin was a small fort at Monk's Corner, and the church, around a mile from Biggin Bridge. This church was a strong brick building that covered the bridge. It also provided cover for a retreat. Biggin Creek is the most northwardly creek that empties into Cooper river. Marion had sent Maham to destroy the Watboo bridge and cut off that route of retreat. Colonel Maham, went to destroy the Watboo bridge but the placement and force of Colonel Coates stopped Maham from reaching the bridge.

Maham stopped and waited for the main body. He was reinforced by Colonel Peter Horry and his men. Horry assumed command and proceeded to the bridge. British cavalry opposed his attempt It was a quick fight but the British were defeated and driven back. Mounted riflemen attacked, broke through the British and took prisoners. Horry then sent a detail to destroy the bridge. Horry was providing cover for the detail when the British returned in force and forced Horry and all of his men, including the bridge detail, to retreat.

Sumter, believing that Coates had marched out to give him battle and posted in a ravine to wait for Coates. The British, however, were bluffing. They had no intention of fighting. Their activities were to gain time and place all the stores they couldn't carry in the church.

Sometime during the night of July 17, around midnight, the British led by Colonel Coates put everything they couldn't carry inside Biggin Church and set it afire. Sentries in Sumter's camp saw the flames and roused Sumter. Coates was heading toward Charlestown and we were hot on the trail. By we, I mean Sumter and his men, Marion and his men and Light Horse Harry Lee with over 500 of his legion. Sumter left his cannon behind instead of having it follow us.

Colonel Light Horse Harry Lee and Colonel Wade Hampton were leading the chase until they got to a fork in the road at the Wadboo River. Colonel Hampton followed the South Carolina Tories (they called themselves Royalists) that had taken the right-hand road. They didn't have any luck because the Tories had already crossed the river and taken all the boats to the other side.

The British had already got to Quinby's Bridge. They began loosening the planks to take them off. When their rear guard was spotted rushing toward the bridge, they left the planks on the bridge so the rear guard could cross. When the British crossed the river, some of them began cooking breakfast and the cavalry unbridled their horses.

When Colonel Light Horse Harry Lee was seen nearing the bridge, Colonel Coates placed the British soldiers into a defense position and had his howitzer posted at the end of the bridge. The howitzer crew didn't fire because some of their own British soldiers were still taking planks from the bridge.

Colonel Hezekiah Maham's dragoons charged through the British soldiers taking planks from the bridge and straight to the howitzer. They drove the howitzer crew from the gun. The charge pushed most of the loosened planks from the bridge and the men who followed them across had to hang on to the bridge stringers. Colonel Maham's horse was shot from under him. Some of the British who had been trying to wreck the bridge picked up their muskets, fired one volley and retreated.

Captain McCauley didn't stop to fight on the bridge. He led his men in a charge that carried the fight to the causeway on the British side. Captain Armstrong led his men right behind McCauley and attacked Colonel Coates. The 19th Regiment of Foot was ordered to form into a line of battle. Many of the British soldiers had taken off their coats and hadn't been able to put them back on. For a change, the British were the ones who were so confused they were running around like a bunch of chickens with their heads cut off.

Colonel Henry "Light Horse Harry" Lee and the rest of his Legion arrived. They immediately started fixing the bridge. They couldn't attack the British defenses because they were only armed with sabers and would be cut down by musket fire before they could reach the British.

Captain McCauley and Captain Armstrong, finding that they were the only ones who made it across the bridge, rode to the rear of the British, where they would be safer there. The two commanders wheeled their men into the woods on the side of the causeway.

The British were too crowded to form a line of battle. Colonel Thomas Taylor had a rifleman with a long range gun. He picked off the British at the bridge. Colonel Taylor and his men then crossed the river. If they had been fighting experienced British soldiers instead of new recruits, the Cavalry of Lee's legion might have been badly defeated. The men in the 19th Regiment of Foot was not battle-hardened veterans. They were untested recruits and not sure what to do.

Lee's Legion caught a hundred men of the British 19th Regiment of Foot about a mile from Quinby's Bridge. The British captain placed his men to receive Lee. Colonel Lee sent Major Eggleston's 2nd Mounted Troop into the woods to flank the British and the rest of the cavalry formed in close order on the road.

The Trumpeter sounded "charge" and the cavalry charged. The British were ordered to shoot and they didn't shoot. I reckon the men in the 19th Regiment of Foot were new or not trained or both because they threw down their muskets without shooting. Lee captured all the baggage and led his men toward Quinby's bridge.

The British retreated into nearby cornfields and ran to find some shelter at Shubrick's Plantation outbuildings. These were owned by Captain Thomas Shubrick, who had been captured at the fall of Charleston. The British forted up their positions at Shubrick's Plantation and waited to be attacked by the Patriots. They only had to wait until late that afternoon. A large force, including troops from Sumter's and Marion's brigades, supported by Lee's Legion, attacked.

The attack went well at first. Then General Sumter's troops ran out of ammunition. When the British realized this , they attacked. Sumter's men were about to be overrun by counter-attacking British troops. General Marion saw this and ordered his men to stop their advance and go help General Sumter's men. The fierce attack my Marion caused the British to retreat to their earlier positions and allowed Sumter's men to retreat. Without ammunition, most of the

Patriots left the battle, letting the British retreat safely to Charlestown.

At Shubrick's Plantation, the British led by Colonel Coates were formed into a square, using the buildings as part of his defense. His only howitzer was placed in the center.

Since they did not have many bayonets, Colonel "Light Horse Harry" Lee and General Francis Marion waited for General Sumter to arrive with artillery. They had a long wait. Sumter did not arrive until after 3 p.m., which allowed the British more time to strengthen their defenses. When Sumter got there, he did not have his cannon. He had left it behind so it would not slow him down.

General Sumter seized command and divided the force into three sections to attack the plantation from three different sides. He put his own brigade in the center. This position gave his men some protection from the plantation's slave buildings. General Marion's brigade was ordered to advance on the right, across open fields with no cover except for a fence about fifty yards in front of the plantation. Marion protested, but Sumter ordered him to attack immediately. Lee's Legion was held in reserve.

Colonel Taylor's riflemen reached the slave quarters. They fired around the corners and drove the British into the house. They started the fight with seven rounds each. It didn't last long. Colonel Taylor and forty-five men rushed up to not more than fifteen paces off the house. Each man screened himself behind a stout fencepost and when the British fired out a window, the riflemen fired back at their enemy. Sometimes a hit a man would fall out the window.

When Taylor's riflemen were out of ammunition, and it didn't take long to fire seven shots each; The British attacked with bayonets. The 19th Regiment of Foot were the attackers. General Marion's men rushed in and helped Taylor's men pull back. Lieutenant Bates of the Camden Company of Mounted Militia was killed after being shot five times. Marion's men suffered greatly.

Major John Baxter was shot off his horse by a musket. He shouted to Colonel Peter Horry that he was wounded. Horry told him to ignore it and stay on his post. Baxter shouted back that he was wounded again. Baxter was shot four times. Fifty of General Marion's men were killed or wounded in this assault.

Colonel Thomas Taylor went looking for General Sumter and found him sitting under the shade of a tree.

General Thomas Sumter,   Public Domain

"General Sumter, I don't know why you sent me forward on a forlorn hope, promising to sustain me and failed to do so, unless you designed to sacrifice me. I will never serve another single hour under you."

The battle lasted three hours and ended when it was too dark to shoot. The darkness was welcomed by General Marion's men since they had also run out of ammunition. Brigadier General Sumter had us retreat three miles to wait for Captain Singleton and the cannon to catch up. That night, all but a hundred of General Marion's men left. Rob and I both stayed. The next day, General Marion and Colonel Henry Lee left General Sumter's command. Both resolved never to fight under Sumter again.

Artist depiction of General Francis Marion, Public Domain

General Sumter withdrew when Colonel Rawdon arrived four miles away. Our casualties for both Quinby's Bridge and Shubrick's Plantation were 30 killed and 30 wounded. The British casualties were six killed, 38 wounded, and 100 captured. The British also lost several wagons, a load of ammunition, and the baggage of the 19th Regiment of Foot. In the baggage was a chest containing 720 guineas. General Sumter took the gold and divided it up among his men.

As far as I'm concerned, Sumter aint worth a dern. They should send him to congress where he might not be able to do us as much harm. At least, he could do no more harm than any other congressman.

11

The Battle of Eutaw Springs

Both Rob and me were glad that Marion made it plain that he would never partner up with Sumter again. Marion led just over a hundred men. We found ourselves riding with three good men, a preacher named John McDaniel, his son also named John McDaniel and Dewey Medlock.

We stayed with Marion and he led us to some high ground with plenty of shade and away from the river and swamp. A good thing to because everyone knows the air above swamps and rivers in July and August can give a man the chills and fever.[8]

As more Tory refugees fled to Charlestown, British and Tory Leaders formed the Troy Refugees into armed units of 400-500 to ravage and loot the Patriot owned farms and plantations. They targeted the area around Charlestown and the rice plantations located around the Combahee River. The idea was to steal rice from the plantations to support the Tory companies and try to discourage the Patriot militias from attacking them, large British

---

[8] Malaria. People weren't to know that malaria was spread by mosquitos for over a hundred years.

forces were sent out. The newly-created dragoon regiment, the SC Light Dragoons, were sent with the foragers to protect them.

Colonel Will Harden reported the problem to General Greene and asked for help stopping them. General Greene gave General Francis Marion the choice of whether or not to help Colonel Harden and Swamp Fox decided to take some mounted men and give him some help.

General Marion sent a force under Captain George Cooper to raise a ruckus between Dorchester and Moncks Corner. He left all his men without horses with Colonel Hezekiah Maham and took Peter Horry's cavalry and around 200 hand-picked men from his brigade. Me and Rob, along with Dewey Medlock, Preacher McDaniel and John McDaniel were riding with him.

General Marion knows how to travel fast. After a quick ride of over one hundred miles, we joined Colonel Will Harden. Colonel Harden had been watching the British and knew now that they were led by a Major Fraser. Harden couldn't take to the take the field, but he sent Major Charles Harden with 80 men with Marion. While we were camped at Horse Shoe, Colonel William Stafford with around one hundred fifty men joined our force.

Marion wanted to attack the British at Godfrey's Savannah on the night of August 26th or maybe it was the 27th. Most of us were ready to go but some lame-brained militia didn't follow orders and Marion had to stop the planned attack.

Marion was some irritated about having to cancel the attack at Godfrey's Savannah. He was irritated but he wasn't quitting. He sent Colonel Peter Horry to Cheraw. He got there to find that three British schooners had been taking on rice, guarded by thirty men. The British were warned about Horry's approach and sailed downriver before Horry got there. They didn't get away with all the rice though.

General Marion sent out other patrols to spy out other British positions but they found the British were too strong for them to attack. Marion then set up an ambush for them on the causeway that led to Parker's Ferry. After dark, he hid men on the causeway to spy the British movements. The British were warned that Marion was close and sent out a patrol to look for General Marion's force. This caused Marion's spies to move off the causeway. The British couldn't find Marion's camp in the dark so they gave up trying and went on to Hyrne's Plantation.

The next morning, General Marion got us up early and we went after the British. We got to Hyrne's Plantation and put us in a line of battle along the tree line. We tried to trick them into charging us so we could ambush them good. We fired a few long-range shots that wounded two British soldiers, but they didn't bite the bait. They weren't tricked into our ambush. We sniped at them for about two hours, then we left and rode back to camp.

I thought it was awful inconsiderate of the British not to fall into our trap after we went to so much trouble setting it up. I mentioned it to Rob and he said he thought so too.

The next day, the British moved to Hayne's Plantation. They weren't by themselves. General Marion followed them again. He was still looking for a fight and set up his camp about five miles away from the British. Two days later, I guess that Marion got tired of waiting because he hid all of us in a swamp alongside the causeway. He moved Colonel Will Harden's men move back about a hundred yards from the ambush line in a reserve for our main attack. Major Sam Cooper and sixty swordsmen were told to attack the British on their rear after they entered the ambush. With all that done, we settled down to wait for the British to come and be ambushed.

The British infantry were led off Hayne's Plantation about mid-afternoon. Two cannon and their crews were leading the column and Major Fraser with his mounted SC Royalists were in the back of the column. It was dern near dark when they stumbled into our ambush. Some of our men fired too soon at the first British they saw. The officer leading the British sent Major Fraser to attack us and drive us off.

Major Fraser sent a lieutenant with some men charging at our line while he put three other divisions on the road, and to the left and right of the road. General Marion's mounted men charged the attacking British and they turned and ran like they were turpentined dogs. Major Fraser believed that the men chasing his lieutenant were Colonel Will Harden's men and ordered his cavalry to charge at full gallop to head us off.

General Marion now had the British right where he wanted them. He blew his whistle and signaled his hidden men. In seconds, we had Major Fraser's horsemen surrounded. When our men were about forty yards away, they opened up with muskets loaded with buck and ball[9] and the British dragoons began falling like fall leaves in a high wind. At a distance of 40 yards, the Patriots opened up with buckshot and the dragoons went down.

Major Fraser rallied his men and ordered a charge. Marion's men shot a second volley followed by a third volley. With his men falling, Fraser decided that there was no way he could attack the s but the Patriots delivered a second volley, and then a third. There was no way for Major Fraser to attack Marion's men in the swamp. He ordered a retreat down the causeway, down the whole length of the ambush. Major Fraser's horse was killed and I guess he got hurt pretty bad because all of the cavalry behind him rode over him. I heard later that over twenty dead British or Tories and over twenty dead horses were found after the ambush was over.

We stayed there on the causeway for three more hours until General Marion was warned that a large group of infantry with a cannon were coming our way. He put all of his riflemen in a hidden

---

[9] Buck and ball is six to twelve .30 or .32 caliber lead balls and one lead ball slightly smaller than the musket's bore.

position and they fired at the cannon crew. They wounded and killed most of the men with the cannon. He could have killed most or all of the SC Royalists with his riflemen but we were too low on ammunition. Of course, most of us hadn't eaten since we set up the ambush more than a day ago so Marion had us all just slip away into the swamp.

General Fraser whipped Major Fraser   Public Domain

We didn't have too many killed or wounded. General Marion lost one man killed and Colonel William Stafford lost three men wounded.

The British decided to leave the area and make tracks as quick as they could back to Charlestown. General Marion sent a party after them. They found forty dead horses on the road. Marion returned "home" with his prisoners.

While Marion was busy whipping Fraser and the "SC Royalist," General Greene was busy too. He called for all of his detachments except for those with Marion, Maham, and Harden to meet him at Friday's Ferry. The travel wasn't easy.

Heavy rain had put all the swamps bordering the Wateree under water. The flooding didn't stop Greene. It barely slowed him down. He went first to Camden and reached Howell's Ferry in Late August. He sent messengers in all directions to order his detachments to join him there. He aimed to cross the river quickly and march on the British.

The British were warned of Greene's moves and fell back to Eutaw Springs. The British army had moved forty miles, by forced marched, from the to get to Eutaw Springs. It tired them a right smart but now it was not possible for Greene to force the British into battle. Knowing this, Greene slowed his chase and moved his army down the south bank of the Congaree River to see what his choices were. He sent Colonel Lee to shadow the British and General Pickens was sent to take a position to spy on the British at Orangeburg.

The British were fooled by the slow progress being made by our army. Greene's deliberateness fooled the British into believing that we weren't real confident. That made it seem, to the British, like a good time to fight us. The British moved the detachment from Fair Lawn to Eutaw Springs and moved the garrison at Orangeburg to Fairlawn to replace them. The British figured they could get away with this because Marion was out of the area. Of course, Marion was busy whipping Fraser.

Captain Cooper was sent to the Cypress swamp, where he routed a bunch of Tories. Afterwards, he moved on down the road where he drove off the cattle from the British fort at Dorchester. Since there was no opposition, he went down the Charlestown road and found a body of Tories in a brick church about twelve miles from the town. He charged the Tories and drove them off. With that accomplished, he turned on to the Goose Creek road and went to the Ten Mile House. He returned and passed over Goose Creek bridge, took a wide swing around the British at Monck's Corner. He arrived in camp at Peyre's plantation to join Marion, who was there with a passel of prisoners.

The very fact that Marion was there and what he had to do to get there deserves to be told - - - and needs to be repeated. General "the Swamp Fox" Marion had moved across the country from St. Stephen's to the Edisto. He took us through both lines of British communication with Charlestown. He led us as we surprised and whipped parties of the British and Tories bigger than us. We returned the same way, passed the Santee safely and delivered our prisoners. Marion then led us to twenty miles below Eutaw Springs to spy on the British and stop their messengers Peyre's plantation and Fair Lawn. When Greene called for Marion to meet him, Marion led us in a circle to pass the British and reach a position on the south side of the Santee to wait for General Greene. All of this was done in a week.

We were wakened early in the morning of the 8th of September. We began moving just shy of four o'clock. Our army moved in four columns. Lee's Legion and the State troops of South Carolina moved out first. The state militia of North Carolina and the militia of South Carolina under Marion and Pickens followed. Behind us were the Continentals or regulars. The last column was Colonel Will Washington's Cavalry and Kirkwood's Delawares. The cannon moved between the columns. This formation was to make it easier for us to form the attack when we arrived at Eutaw Springs.

The British had moved to Eutaw Springs. The British, at Eutaw Springs, had been warned that Greene's aimed to attack them while Colonel Stuart was on the way to meet a convoy of provisions coming from Charlestown. Colonel Stuart had arrived at Eutaw Springs and rested there. He believed that Greene would have to wait for Marion to join him. He didn't know that Marion had already returned and was only seventeen miles away.

We didn't know it until later, but two men from the North Carolina militia had deserted and were on their way to warn the British at Eutaw Springs. Two hours after we began our move to Eutaw Springs, the two deserters from the North Carolina militia reported to the British that Greene was on his way to attack. The British commander didn't believe them and instead of rewarding them, sent them to prison. Not only didn't he believe them, he sent out an unarmed rooting party[10] of over a hundred men with a twelve man armed guard.

Before the rooting party had been gone an hour, the British received word from one of their patrols that Greene and his army were about four miles away. The patrol was only two hundred men and when they discovered our advance, they charged at us. From the quickness of their attack, it was plain that they had no idea how strong our advance was or that the biggest part of Greene's army was behind the advance.

The Battle of Eutaw Springs, Public Domain

Meeting and whipping the British attack was no big thing.

---

[10] A rooting party was a group of men sent out to dig up potatoes, sweet potatoes, turnips and other root crops.

The sound of the firing brought the rooting party out retreating back to their camp. We captured them all. A few of the British cavalry escaped and we had to figure that they were on the way to warn the British commander.

The British pushed up a bunch of infantry about a mile from Eutaw Springs. Their orders were to fight us and slow us down while the British at Eutaw Springs formed the men and prepared for battle. Greene took the attack by the patrol to mean that the British were close. He stopped, had rum rations given to the men and formed his order of battle. I took my ration of rum with a lot of water and went with Rob to spy out where the British were.

Greene's order of battle put the militia on the front line. He put the South Carolinians on the left and the right sides flanking the North Carolina militia in the middle. General Marion commanded the right, General Pickens the left, and Colonel Malmedy the center. Colonel Henderson with State troops covered the left of this line, and Colonel Lee with his Legion covered the right.

The second line was the Continental Soldiers. The Maryland, North Carolina and Virginia lines and two three-pounders formed the second line. Colonel Will Washington and his corps were kept in the rear as the reserve.

The Continentals were more than eager to fight. A sight more than eager because they wanted to prove to everyone, maybe mostly to themselves, that their actions at Hobkirk's Hill were more accident than commonplace.

I have been told that the army moved forward in this order. When they met the British advance, they drove them off like a big hound chasing rabbits. The British were one line, across the Congaree or River road. The ground was a bit higher in front of his encampment, which was not far from Eutaw Springs. Major Majoribanks with the flank battalion was on the right, a hundred paces from Eutaw Creek. Cruger's corps was in the center, and the Sixty-third and Sixty-fourth were on the left. The British left was without any natural cover. The British reserve was Major Coffin with his cavalry and a detachment of infantry hidden behind a thick hedge.

The British right had protection from a thick thicket in front of them.

We went in from the west. We cleared away the skirmishing parties and our men attacked with a fierceness that bordered on rashness. Our men charged and fought well. Two of our cannon and one of the British cannon were hit and put out of action. The North and South Carolina militias attacked the British regulars in front of them steadily and without showing fear. Later, both General Greene and the British praised their conduct. They attacked like they were von Steuben trained Continentals.[11] Considering the number of successful attacks that Marion has made, I don't think that anyone should have been surprised. After all, less than two weeks earlier we had whipped Fraser and his bunch. General Pickens was leading Sumter's men and they were experienced too. The North Carolina militia in the middle were not the experienced veterans that the South Carolinians were. When the British veterans of the Sixty-third and Sixty-fourth regiments of the British line charged with their bayonets, the North Carolina militia was pushed back, forcing Marion's and Pickens' militia on their flanks to retreat.

From the start of the fight, our covering parties on the right and left had been fighting steadily. The Legion's cavalry had not been in the enemy's fire, but the State troops under Henderson had been in the most exposed situation in the field. The American right, with the additions of the Legion infantry, had extended beyond the British left. This was not the case on our left. The American left fell far short of the

---

[11] *General Greene expressed his admiration of the firmness exhibited on this occasion by these men, writing to Steuben, "such conduct would have graced the veterans of the great King of Prussia."*

British right. This left the State troops exposed to the volley fire of a large part of the British right. Our left was particularly exposed to the fire of the British right. That British position was well led and commanded. The punishment our left took put a strain on their good intentions and resolve. Henderson wanted permission to charge the British right and sent his request to Greene to be allowed to charge the British and get rid of the source of their aggravation. General Greene didn't think they should run the risk of leaving our cannons and militia open to flanking fire. Their flanks would have been left uncovered if the charge had been made and was defeated. While waiting for the orders to attack, Henderson was bad wounded.

Henderson being bad wounded shook up his soldiers and it took a bit to get them straightened out. Colonel Wade Hampton came up and straightened things out. He was helped by Colonel Polk and Colonel Mydelton. Like I said, Colonel Wade Hampton was a fighting South Carolinian.

After the militia fell back, partly because their center was forced back and partly because they needed more ammunition, the force of the battle hit the Continentals of the second line, and Sumner's North Carolina brigade on the right. They held although outnumbered and were having volleys directed at them. It took a while but the larger numbers of the British caused them to give and fall back. Their falling back just tickled the British to death. They figured that the Americans were whipped and began rushing forward. All their excitement did was mess up their line. Greene saw that their line was messed up and sent Colonel Williams and his men to advance with bayonets and sweep the field. The Virginia and Maryland Continentals went into action and attacked. I reckon that they were attacking both the British and the memory of what had happened at Hobkirk's Hill. When they were about forty yards from the British, the Virginians halted and fired a volley that rocked the British. The British confusion caused the whole second line of Continentals to charge the

British.

When the Americans charged, the left of the British army fell back, retreating and acting like addled chickens. Light Horse Harry saw this and took advantage of the British confusion. He wheeled his infantry and attacked the enemy's exposed and broken flank. This served to increase the confusion and disorder.

The British Center stood firm waiting for the attack that they knew was coming. They knew they outnumbered us and were convinced they could outfight us.

Our Continentals attacked with the confidence that they could win and a bucket full of bravery. The British regulars met them as you would expect British regulars to do. It was bayonet against bayonet and sword against sword. Both sides figured they would win.

The problem for the British regulars was the rest of their line was giving way and exposing their flanks. Their retreat pushed back their own center. While this was going on, the Marylanders stopped on command and delivered volleys into the British line. The British line, except for the right side, yielded. Our soldiers were shouting and sure of victory now. The trouble for us began when some of our soldiers started going hog wild and pig crazy.

Added to our problems, Lee was with his infantry instead of his cavalry. His cavalry should have attacked then and routed the already retreating British but without Lee leading them, they did nothing.

General Greene saw that the British right must be moved and sent me to tell Colonel Will Washington and Colonel Wade Hampton to attack the British right. I galloped to Washington and he rode into action at once, without waiting for Hampton to join him. Washington's cavalry galloped through the woods and into the action. I reached Colonel Hampton and he took his men toward the action. I returned to General Greene to let him know that his orders were delivered. Hampton made for the creek, trying to support Washington's left. Before Hampton got there, Washington charged the British right. The thicket he tried to charge through was thicker than he had thought and broke up his charge. Washington turned to his left and tried to join Hampton in attacking between the creek and the British. This exposed their flank to the British. The British directed mass volleys at their charge and brought down a lot of our cavalry. They wounded Colonel Washington and captured him. Only two of Washington's officers came away without being killed or wounded.

Colonel William Washington, Public Domain

The survivors of Washington's charge were rallied under two

younger officers, Lieutenant Gordon and Cornet Simons. They joined Hampton and they charged the British again. The attack failed but Kirkwood and his Delawares charged the British. They had better luck than the cavalry had. They pushed the British line back with the rest of the British.

The British army retreated through their camp. The tents were still standing and the soldiers food and extra equipment was there for everyone to see. While some of our soldiers grabbed everything that tempted them, the army came under fire the windows of a house, surprising the American line with heavy, volleyed fire. Their confusion was so bad that the Legion's infantry was the only bunch that wasn't shaken.

General Greene, and most of his officers, didn't know that too many of the soldiers and militia had been distracted by the chance to loot and plunder the British camp. General Sumter had long had the policy that his soldiers could keep plunder since they usually didn't get paid by the state. Other soldiers saw the looting and plundering going on and decided to join it. Many had outran their officers in chasing the British and it got out of control quick.

General Greene sent word for Colonel Lee to take his cavalry and attack the British cavalry that was protecting their line. When the messenger reached Lee's corps, he discovered that Lee was with his infantry. He gave the message to Major Eggleston and the major got the cavalry moving into action and they attacked as ordered. Their attack was pushed back and was not successful. .

When General Greene realized that Major Eggleston's attack failed, he ordered a retreat. The British cavalry saw the retreat forming and decided to hit us again. He charged his cavalry at our rear, most of which was spread out still looting the British camp.

I heard someone saying "damn, damn, damn" then realized that it was me. I noticed that Rob was beside me and he was cussing too. Rob ripped a cartridge paper with his teeth and rammed it down his musket barrel. I could see by the size that it was a buck and ball cartridge. I started to remind him to prime his pan by the was already priming from his horn. I raised my rifle, took a close aim and fired. While I was reloading, Rob rode closer to the British where his musket could do more damage.

Rob looked like he was going to try to stop the British attack on our rear by himself. I spurred my horse up beside him to - - - well, I'm not sure what I aimed to do because the two of us couldn't have stopped the British attack no matter how much we wanted to stop it. Fortunately, we didn't have to stop it by ourselves.

Over the shooting, cussing and other battle noises, I heard yelling like a hundred banshees were holding a party. The yelling came from our troops and was headed for the British.

The British cavalry aimed to spread destruction on our rear but they didn't reckon on Colonel Wade Hampton. Greene had told Hampton to cover our retreat. Hampton saw what was going on and ordered a charge. He and his men charged, yelling like there was five thousand of them - - - which there wasn't. The fighting was right sharp with neither Hampton's men nor the British wanting to give an inch. Before long, the British had to back off. Hampton's cavalry wasn't ready to quit fighting and they continued to fight until they were close enough for the British line to fire some volleys at them that did a lot of damage. Colonel Hampton rallied his men, and pulled them back to his station on the border of the woods. While this was being done, the British captured all the cannons that we had left on the field.

I may be wrong but I don't think we would have lasted an hour as an army if Hampton hadn't charged the British like he did and if his men hadn't fought like they did. One thing I was sure of is that Rob hadn't been of any mind to retreat and I wasn't going to leave him. If it hadn't been for Hampton, me and Rob would have been killed or captured sure as coal is black.

If Hampton had saved the day for us, then the British commander who had been holding the line stopped us from whipping the British that day. That officer (I heard his name was Majoribanks) had held our left back and even captured Colonel Will Washington. That British officer took advantage of every opening we gave him. As Greene withdrew his army in an orderly retreat, the British officer ordered an attack on all the Americans still looting their camp. The men looting the camp had to either leave the camp or be killed or captured.

Some of the men looting the camp were killed and some were captured. Most of the rest rallied around Colonel Hampton. They were preparing a defense and were looking for a chance to counterattack the British but the British decided they were too crippled up to leave the shelter of their cover and attack us.

General Greene stopped long enough to gather all our wounded that we could reach and make arrangements to bury our dead. He left Colonel Wade Hampton with his soldiers on the field and fell back to Burdell's plantation about seven miles away. He had to fall back to Burdell's plantation because there was no other place with a water supply big enough to support his army.

I felt just like I had felt at Guilford Courthouse. I wasn't sure who had won the battle. I didn't feel whipped and neither did any of the men around me but we were retreating. I was pretty sure we had hurt the British a sight more than we had been hurt but our Army was retreating.

Rob sure didn't feel whipped. He was ready to attack the British again. More important, I'm not sure that the British soldiers felt like they had won.

On one hand, I thought that a commander like General Daniel Morgan could have led the army to a clear victory. On the other hand, I figured that General Nathaniel Greene had left the field with his army in better shape and with fewer men killed, wounded or captured than General Morgan would have. I guess the important thing is that neither me nor the army felt beaten.

Major General Nathaniel Greene, by Charles Wilson Peale, Public Domain

When things had calmed down a bit, I rode over to Colonel

Hampton.

"Colonel Hampton, you and your men did a real good job."

"Who might you be?"

"Nate Bowman, Colonel Hampton, of King's Mountain, the Cowpens, Guilford Courthouse and a sight of other skirmishes and battles. Here lately, mostly I spy for General Greene."

"I believe I've heard of you. What do you have to offer today?"

"I believe, when it gets dark, that I can get closer to the British and find out what is going on with them."

"What if you get caught?"

"I hope I don't."

"What do you expect to find out?"

"I expect to find out what they aim to do tomorrow, maybe what they aim to do tonight."

"How do you intend to get close?"

"I'll take two of their wounded back to the British."

We talked and I explained my plan. Colonel Hampton finally nodded.

"Might work, might not work."

"Worth a try, I guess."

"Do it, good luck."

I handed him my rifle, pouch and powder horn. "Could you make sure my rifle is taken care of until I get back?"

"You'll need to have a gun."

"I'll pick up one of the old muskets."

I picked up an old Brown Bess that had seen a lot of wear and a cartridge box. I waited until I saw prisoners being moved, took a deep breath and moved.

I went to one of the small groups of prisoners being ushered in and picked two prisoners who looked able to walk without help. I turned to the guard who looked like he was in charge.

"I need to take these two prisoners to General Greene so he can ask them questions."

"Are you sure?"

"What do you think I'm going to do? Do you think I'll take them back to the British or something?"

"I guess not."

I took the two prisoners and a long rope. I tied each of their wrists to different ends of the rope and took the middle of the rope in my left hand and mounted my horse. I kneed my horse and rode to the edge of our lines with the prisoners. When we were outside of our lines, I glanced back and saw Colonel Hampton wave at me. I turned to the prisoners and asked, "Do you men want to go back to your army?"

"What?"

"Do you men want to go back to your army?"

"Yes!"

"Then walk fast and as soon as we get past that oak, run!"

As we got to the oak, I heard a shout behind us and several musket shots. I shouted to the two British soldiers to run and we made tracks. Within five hundred yards, a British patrol met us and took us to their lines.

When we got through their sentries, Three British soldiers dragged me from my horse and I received several punches and had my hands tied before I was pulled over to a British captain.

"What have you got to say for yourself Rebel?"

"I want to be on the winning side."

"Change sides as soon as you get caught is hardly what we

want."

"I didn't get caught. I took two British prisoners and brought them with me."

The captain walked away and returned in about fifteen minutes.

"Untie him."

I was untied and led to four other British officers. They looked as tired as I felt but more uncomfortable. I didn't grudge them their uniforms a bit.

"I understand you're tired of being a rebel."

"I never did like it much. I was afraid that if I didn't join them, they would hang me."

"They probably would have, bloody rebels. What is your name?"

"Nate."

"Nate who."

"Nate Bowman."

"How long have you been with the rebels?"

"Since February, I think."

"Aren't you sure?"

"February, I'm pretty sure."

An hour and a half of questioning later and they seemed to be satisfied. I gave them some information, nothing important but enough to make it seem like I was trying to be helpful. While this was going on, I tried to make it seem like I was paying all of my attention to them. Of course I wasn't! I could hear soldiers breaking muskets and throwing them into the springs. I could hear the sounds of an army getting ready to move and it didn't sound like they were getting ready to attack.

They were going to pull back. I figured they were probably

going back to Charlestown. I continued to weave reasons to join the British into my answers. I told them that I had been told that every American that joined them would get a plantation when the British won the war. They made promises that I didn't think they could keep and I pretended to believe every word they said.

Then someone came with orders and things got real busy. I moved off and started helping some other destroy supplies. I could see that they were destroying everything they couldn't carry with them. I heard that the British commanders, a Colonel Stuart, had sent to Fairlawn for help and that his army would be leaving before dawn to meet the reinforcements.

When it got darker, I slipped into the brush and stayed out of sight. After a while, there was a ruckus as some British soldiers were looking for someone. It didn't take me long to figure out that they were looking for me. I lay low and stayed quiet. When some British soldiers and Tory militia began going through the brush where I was hiding, I joined them and wasn't noticed. When we got to the outer line of pickets, I again stepped into the shadows and moved away from the British camp.

Soon, everyone was moving. The pickets were being pulled back and soon, the whole army was moving except for a patrol that was continuing to make sure the supplies were destroyed and, I suspected, looking for me. . I stayed where I was until the sun was coming up, then made my way toward Colonel Hampton's lines.

I told Hampton what I had learned and suspected. He sent a courier to General Greene with the news. General Greene had been readying his army to attack the British. Now he was told that the British had pulled out and there was no one to attack.

General Greene put his army on the move from Burdell's plantation, and followed the British army for a pretty good piece. The British didn't slow down and showed no eagerness to fight Greene's army. Seeing this, Greene stopped and sent General Marion and Colonel Lee with their men to go around the retreating British army and get between it and the reinforcements from Fairlawn. It might have worked but the British were retreating a sight faster than we thought. They moved a good fifteen miles before they stopped and by that time, they were within a few miles of their reinforcements.

Colonel Lee and Colonel Maham caught up with the retreating British the next day and attacked. Major Eggleston attacked the British while Colonel Lee moved to attack the British front.

Major Eggleston had to move through thick black jack oaks. This slowed them down enough for the British to form and fire. The British then moved to keep on retreating. Major Eggleston's horse was killed. The major was not hit but it is said that he had five bullet holes in his clothes and gear.

Colonel Lee and his men had a little better luck. The British left behind wagons that were found to be filled with wounded men. Colonel Lee allowed the wounded to continue on behind the retreating British army.

General Marion later reported that he captured 24 British and 4 Tories.

Marion and Lee had planned to meet at Ferguson's Swamp and get between the two British forces but the British were moving so fast that they got there first. The British only stopped when they reached Wantoot, Daniel Ravenel's plantation which was a good twenty miles from Eutaw Springs. Somewhere during all this moving, General Greene got a message from Governor Burke of North Carolina. The message was that he was move north of the Santee River unless he was attacked. General Greene was to stay in a position to oppose General Cornwallis in case Cornwallis was able to leave Virginia and return to the Carolinas.

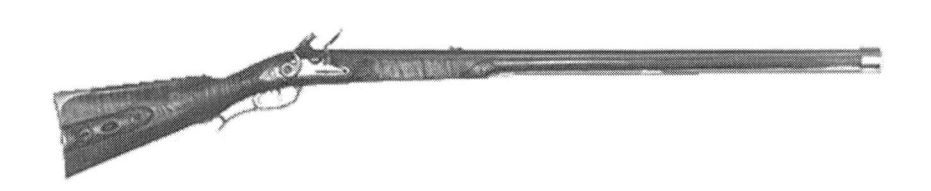

General Greene took his army back to the High Hills of the Santee to rest and recover. The British had been in such a hurry to retreat that they left around seventy-five wounded and most of their dead was unburied. We later learned that the British officer who had held his position at Eutaw Springs, Major Majoribanks, had been wounded and died of those wounds before the British reached Charlestown.

The British army appeared to be preparing to meet General Cornwallis's army and help it return to Charlestown. General Greene began gathering all the help he could to stop Cornwallis when he returned.

It looked like things were getting exciting.

12

Camp Follower Gossip
October 25, 1781

I've got to say that resting in the High Hills of the Santee was nice. Not as nice as it would have been at my home with my wife close to me but it was nice to be high enough to catch a breeze and away from the disease filled air around the swamps.

I had been thinking of how nice it would be to have my wife closer but I'd seen what the camp followers had to put up with and I knew she was better off on our farm protected by our sons and kinfolk. I knew, even if I didn't say it out loud, that I was looking for an excuse to leave the army for a spell and go back to my wife and family.

Rob's wife, Anne, was as changeable as the wind. One minute she was crying because she couldn't have him close enough and the next she was telling him to get out of her way and to stay gone.

I'd heard of women acting that way when they were with

child but I'd never been this close to it. They were coming to the fire I'd just put a big kettle of stew on and she was trying again to straighten Rob out.

"I don't know why you go off from me and stay gone so long."

"You told me to. You told me to go and not to come back!"

"Well I didn't mean not to come back to be for so long. You and Nate were gone for three days. Do you think I got nothing better to do than worry about you while I'm carrying your baby?"

"I thought it was our baby."

"Don't you go sassing me! If it hadn't been for you I wouldn't be carrying a baby now."

"But you said . . . . . ."

"Don't you go but you said - but you said - but you said - to me. I know what I meant."

I figured it was time to rescue Rob so I stood up and took her hand.

"Anne, you look tuckered out. Why don't you sit in my seat while Rob goes to get us water for tea?"

"Thank you Nate, your wife is sure a lucky woman. I keep telling all the widows that they should find a man like you."

"Anne, you did tell them I have a wife, didn't you?"

"Yes - - - I guess so."

I was ready to bet that she hadn't. That would explain all the attention I had got from the widowed camp followers. I was going to have to talk to Rob about that.

By the time that Rob returned with water for tea, Anne's ma and a crowd of camp followers were gathered around the fire. It was getting toward evening and there was a little chill in the air, not much but just enough to make the fire feel nice. The stew was bubbling and some of the women were laying out bread and offering suggestions.

"Nate, don't you think we should put some potatoes in the stew?"

"In about an hour, I'm going to put in some rice. You can add some onions and seasoning if you want to."

That led to the women talking about what seasoning to add and how much, how thick or thin to slice the onions and what else they should do. I've never seen it to fail. If women are doing something, every single one of them has to comment on everything.

Right then, I didn't mind. I pulled a small jug out and motioned to Rob. When he came over, I poured two mugs almost full; of hot tea and added the whiskey. I broke a cinnamon stick in half and put a piece in each mug and added a dash of nutmeg. After a few sips, we stirred in some molasses. It wasn't bad.

I added the rice and stirred the stew when it was time. I let the women do the seasoning. I decided to let them do the stirring to and Rob fixed us another whiskey and tea. Feeling generous, I let the women do the serving too. I was content to drink whiskey, eat stew and wait for the women to start gossiping.

I didn't have to wait long. A woman named Debora started.

"Did you hear what happened down to Monks Corner a few weeks ago?"

"What did you hear?"

"Hezekiah Maham and his Light Dragoons caught around a hundred prisoners below Moncks Corner. They did it right in plain sight of the British army too. I think it was by Fair Lawn Plantation. Not only that, I was talking to a man from the Watauga who was there. He said he served under Captain Roger Topp of Sullivan County, Colonel Isaac Shelby, and Colonel Anthony Bledsoe were commanding. They were helped out by Colonel John Sevier and

Colonel Robertson too. They crossed over the Santee River and joined General Marion with Colonel Horry and. Colonel Maham of the Cavalry. We were spying on the British and sure pestering the British. He said they took their Hospital and about a hundred prisoners at Moncks Corner."

"That sounds about right."

"Well tell me Nate, how come General Greene aint winning no victories?"

I raised my hand to let them know that I was thinking and thought about it. When I had my thoughts ready, I told them what I thought.

Nate's thoughts:

We've been fighting for our independence from England since April 1775. We've not had a lot of victories. There was Trenton, Princeton, and Saratoga but we lost more battles than we won.

From what I hear, the battle of Monmouth was a draw. The next year, we lost Savannah and in 1780, we lost trying to take Savannah. We won a lot of small scrapes but no big battles - - - not that I know of anyhow. Gates showed how great he aint at Camden and dern near lost his whole army. We've had some clear victories. Some big victories like at King's Mountain and, the Battle of the Cowpens. We took Fort Watson, Fort Motte, Augusta and some other places and we didn't win at Camden or Ninety-Six. Both Camden and Ninety-Six were abandoned and destroyed.

That brings us a question. Should we lose trying to kill British when we can wait a spell and they will leave? I figure Eutaw Springs was a draw but the British couldn't leave fast enough and destroyed over a thousand Brown Bess muskets and a sight of supplies and provisions before they ran off. The way they ran off - - - I aint sure they won anything.

Another question I've got is this one. How long should a victory last? Summer of 1780, the British captured Charlestown and their dragoons and light infantry ran all over South Carolina all the way up to the border of North Carolina. Then our congress sent us Gates who some thought was a smart fighting general. I've yet to find anybody now who says Gates was worth a dern. General Marion and other militia were doing damage to the British and Tories but the first clear win we got was at King's Mountain. After King's Mountain, The British were knocked back on their heels and it got worse for them at the Battle of the Cowpens. Cornwallis chased Greene and his army all the way to Virginia but it was Cornwallis had to leave the Carolinas.

General Greene got here last December and the first thing he had to do was straighten out the supply mess. He made sure we got clothing, supplies, provisions and more men. He had to move most of his command away from Charlotte to Cheraw and sent General Morgan west with around six hundred men. I've been told this aint the usual way things are done.

General Greene didn't sit on his hands. He prepared for a fast retreat if it came to needing one. He sent men to learn everything they could about the main rivers in North Carolina; the Catawba, Yadkin, and Dan. He had the men he sent gather all the boats, barges and ferries. That way, if he had to retreat, his army could cross the rivers quickly and the British would have to go upstream to the nearest ford before they could go back to chasing General Greene. Cornwallis didn't think about those things. He sent his most brutal cavalry commander, Tarleton, to attack General Morgan. Tarleton moved quick and Morgan retreated. I aint sure that he was really retreating. I think he had picked out the place he wanted to fight. Morgan set his men up the way he wanted at Hannah's Cowpens and waited for Tarleton. We all know what happened there.

Tarleton was in such a big hurry to attack Morgan that his men got no breakfast and were moving at four in the morning. When they got to Morgan, Tarleton ordered them to attack. Morgan's riflemen killed a bunch of them and fell back. The militia shot two volleys and moved back just like they had been told to do. Colonel Howard's Continentals stood like giants and the militia that had pulled back helped. Will Washington's cavalry smashed the British like a watermelon hit by a club. Tarleton ordered his dragoons to attack and they refused. Almost a thousand of Tarleton's command were killed, wounded, or captured.

General Greene led his army in a retreat all the way into Virginia. In Virginia, Greene got supplies, provisions and reinforcements. In North Carolina, Cornwallis declared victory without getting more supplies, provisions or reinforcement.

Greene went back to North Carolina and they fought to a draw at Guilford Courthouse. At that time, there were British posts all the way from Charlestown to Ninety-Six and down to Augusta and Savannah. Now that line of posts is gone. We didn't capture all of them but the ones we didn't capture, they had to abandon.

Now, you ask why we lost at Eutaw Springs. Well, I was at Eutaw Springs and I don't feel whipped. I'd say the fight was a draw and the British run away faster and farther than we did. At Guilford Courthouse and at Eutaw Springs, the British lost more men than they could recover.

They declared victory but they didn't whip us.

Greene has driven Cornwallis into Virginia where we hear he's penned up by General Washington and the French. He ran Rawdon back to Charlestown where he decided he was too sick to stay and he left for England only to be captured by the French Navy. Now he's driven the British back into Charlestown.

General Greene has beaten two or three British armies without himself winning a single battle! As long as he keeps doing this, I don't care if he ever wins a battle!

By now the camp followers had found the jugs and had used the whiskey to sweeten their tea. One, and I aint sure of her name, asked, "Nate, what about Bloody Bill Cunningham and his men? Aint they going around killing men, women and children?"

"That's what I've heard. I figure that local militias will tend to them."

"What will you be doing, Nate?"

"I'm going to leave the army for a spell and go back to my farm and family."

I turned to Rob and told him, "Rob, you and your wife and her ma can ride along with me if you want."

"Thank you Nate. When will we leave?"

"Let's give it a week. I want to hear what happened in Virginia before we leave."

Epilogue

I figured I'd about done my due, at least for a spell - - - probably until spring, and set out for home. It had been too long since I had been alone with my wife and family - - - well mostly too long since I'd been alone with my wife. Rob and his wife, Anne, and Anne's ma were with me. Rob had agreed to work with me until spring, then he would decide if he should go back to help General Greene or stay close to his wife.

Rob hadn't said anything about going back to his pa's farm and I didn't guess that he would. He wasn't the same man that had left there in January. Rob's opinion of his pa hadn't been too high when he left and I reckoned it had dropped a right smart.

We got to my farm two days later, Dan Bowman rode up on Buford. I was as glad to see him as he was to see me. He stayed a few days to rest his horse and himself. He told us all about the Battle of Yorktown and we told him what he missed in South Carolina. When he left, me and Rob rode a day a day and a half with him. Dan was in a hurry to get back to his woman Sally and Rob was in a hurry to get back to Anne before she birthed.

As for me, I don't aim to ever leave my wife again. Not if I can help it.

About the Author

Charles E. Hayes served in the United States Air Force for 24 years, retiring as a Master Sergeant with a Master's Degree in Education. His military service included 14 years overseas and two bases in Southeast Asia and two bases in Europe. After leaving the Air Force, he taught for seven years. He is an avid researcher and re-enactor as well as a full-time patriot. When not helping veterans and veterans' families with the Keavy Kentucky chapter of the Disabled American Veterans (D.A.V.), he writes full time.

Books by Charles E. Hayes

Out of the Jungle

The Sword of Gideon

The life and Times of Ralph Marcum

Ambush at the Blue Licks

The Bloody Sevens

Boonesborough Attack

The Longhunter

Blood Debt

Tomahawk Days

Kentucky Tales from the Old Man

Listening to Night Winds at Blue Licks

Kentucky Memories

Jimmy and Tommy Make Soap

Blood on King's Mountain

The War Trail

River Race

Victory

Riding With The Swamp Fox

Rise and Fight

REVOLUTIONARY WAR PENSION APPLICATIONS

The following Revolutionary War pension applications were taken from http://revwarapps.org/index.htmv **This is a wonderful website.** Currently 381 Roster Transcriptions and 21,729 Pension Applications or Bounty Land Claims have been posted in this database including 2490 transcripts made from the online collection of the Library of Virginia and 5 transcripts made from the online collection of the South Carolina Department of Archives & History.

Pension Application of **John Rigby** S9057 Transcribed and annotated by C. Leon Harris

State of North Carolina } Court of Pleas & Quarter Sessions August Term 1832 Duplin County } On this 28 day of August 1832 personally appeared in open Court, the Court aforesaid now in th session Jno Rigby a resident in the county and state aforesaid sixty nine years of age who being first duly sworn according to Law doth on his Oath make the following Declaration in order to obtain the benefit of the Act of Congress passed 7 June 1832 th That he entered the service of the United States under the following named officers and served as herein stated In the year 1780 he entered in the County of Duplin and served with him three tours of three months each during this service he marched from Duplin County to Cross Creek now Fayetteville thence to Grassey Island on Pee Dee River [Grassy Islands at Anson and Richmond counties] thence to Camden South Carolina where the troops to which he belonged joined Genl [Horatio] Gates Army Was in the Battle of Camden [16 Aug 1780] when Gen'l Gates was defeated after that retreated back into North Carolina afterward joined Capt Loves [James Love's] Company & served another tour of three months during which term went to New Hanover County & served the immediate country when Capt Love was surprised & killed at Alex'r Rouses house [Rouse's Tavern in Mar 1781] at the little Bridge above Wilmington. That he again entered the service under Capt James Gillespie as a Volunteer in the Light Horse & served under him three tours of three months each most of this tour he was engaged in scouring the country in pursuit of the Tories his Company of Light Horse was attached to Col. James Kenan's Regiment. And he further Declares that he resided in the County of Duplin at the time he entered the service aforesaid and that he still resides there. He hereby relinquishes every claim to a pension or annuity except the present and declares that his name is not on the pension roll of the Agency of any State [signed] John Rigby Questions propounded by the Court. 1 . Where and in what year were you born st Answer. I was born in the County of Duplin on the 9 of May 1768. th 2 Have you any record of your age & if so where is it. nd Answer. I have & it is at home 3 . Where were you living when called into service Where have you lived since and where rd do you now live Answer In the County of Duplin 4 How were you called into service th Answer I have already detailed that as fully as I can 5 State the names of some of the regular officers who were with the troops where you th served & such Continental & Militia Regiments as you can recollect & the general circumstances of your services. Answer. I recollect Capt. Benj. Coleman & Capt Joseph Rhodes Gen'l. Williams Col. Caswells [Richard Caswell's] Regiment & others. I have already stated as many details as I remember 6 Did you ever receive a discharge from the service if so by whom was it given & what th has become of it. Answer. I received several discharges from Capt. Love & Gillespie they have been burned in my house about 25 years ago 7 State the names of persons to whom you are known in the neighbourhood you live in & th who can testify as to your character for veracity & their belief of your services as a soldier of the Revolution. Answer. Col. Thomas Kenan Thomas Philips John Walkins Esqr & Hugh McCann Esqr. 8 . Is there a Clergyman in your neighbourhood. The Answer. There is not.

Pension application of **George Reed** R8658   fn20NC
Transcribed by Will Graves   rev'd 12/21/09

State of Indiana, Warrick County On this 7th day of October A.D. 1847 personally appears in open court before the Circuit court now sitting George Reed a resident of Warrick County in the state of Indiana aged Eighty Seven Years who first duly sworn according to law doth upon his oath make the following declaration in order to obtain the benefit of the act of Congress passed June 7th 1832. That he entered the service of the United States under the following officers & served as herein stated. From old age & from the great length of time that has elapsed since the happening of the circumstances which he herein relates, he cannot with certainty state the exact period of time but he believes that it was in the summer & as he believes was in the year 1780 that he volunteered into the militia of North Carolina in Onslow County of North Carolina for the term of three months. That the company into which he volunteered was mounted & that this was the only company of mounted men in the regiment to which he belonged. His officers were Col. Thomas Bloodworth [sic, Thomas Bludworth], Maj. James Love, & his Captain was Capt. John McLamma. During this term of his service, the headquarters of his regiment was at Bluford's Bridge on the Cape Fear River in North Carolina & about 10 or 12 miles from Wilmington at which time the British held that place. The most of his time was spent during this term of his service in scouting & in trying to prevent the foraging parties of the British from coming into the country. A part of the time he was engaged in guarding & feeding the cattle of the American troops. About twenty days before this term of his service was ended, he with five others viz. John Wilkins, John Ferrell, Sandy Rouse, John Loper & William Bowen were staying all night on the Edenton Road about 12 or 13 miles from Wilmington at the widow Colier's house with some cattle which they were driving to headquarters for the use of the American troops. On the same night, a detachment of American troops was staying at Rouse's house on the same road & about four miles toward Wilmington from where he was staying with his five companions. On this night, a party of British commanded by Majors

Craig & Manson attacked this detachment of Americans & defeated them. Major James Love, Capt. John McLamma1 with several men were killed.2

      1 This name looks more like "John McClaney" in the power of attorney Reed signed on Sept. 20, 1853

Among them was John Ferrell, the father of one of the men that was with this declarant. Also among the killed was the quartermaster & a lieutenant whose names he has forgotten. A part of this same detachment of British, on the same night, attacked him & his companions at the widow Colier's house &, after a short resistance, they were all taken prisoner by the British. He received from this skirmish two wounds from a bayonet; one on the side & one in the leg below the knee. William Bowen was mortally wounded by a bayonet thrust in the neck & died the next day. This same party of British, on the same night, took one Col. Arnett a prisoner at the house of John Spears' house where he was there lying sick. This Col. Arnett had, before the war, been a treasurer or

2 This same incident is described in the pension application of Benjamin Taylor R10406. See this index. The incident is thought to occurred at Rouse's Tavern sometime in March 1781.

collector for the King & he always understood that there was a reward offered for Col. Arnett. He saw him the next day as they took him in a carriage to Wilmington where he, Col. Arnett, died in about a week afterwards. On the next day, just before night, this declarant was, with his other companions, set free on parole & under a promise to the British Major to go into Wilmington & "take protection". This promise they all violated except Sandy Rouse who, he heard, did "take protection" to save his property. This declarant was hauled in an oxcart to his father's which was about forty miles from Wilmington. The wound in his side was dressed by Col. Thomas Bludworth who was a doctor & when he probed it he said it had penetrated to the hollow, this wound, however, soon got well but his wound in the leg below the knee was sore for a long time, the bone was injured by the bayonet & ever since that time his leg has occasionally broken out causing him a great deal of pain & loss of time & this declarant was unable to serve the balance of his term for which he had volunteered which was about twenty days. In the next spring & as soon as the wound in his leg would permit he again volunteered in the same county into the militia of North Carolina. His officers were Col. Johnson, Maj. Snead & Capt. Zepheriah Ward. This term he was posted & served his whole term at Bluford's Bridge where his regiment was again posted. About two months after the expiration of this second term of service, he again volunteered into the militia of North Carolina in the same county of Onslow for another term of three months. His officers were Col. John Spicer; the man at whose house Col. Arnett was taken, Maj. Ephraim Battle & Capt. Amos Love & for about two three weeks was again posted at Bluford's Bridge when that post was taken command of by a regular officer by the name of Rutherford [Griffith Rutherford] & who he thinks was a general & the regiment of Col. Spicer was sent onto the Edenton Road where he stayed until the British evacuated Wilmington, when he was sent home on furlough he stayed at home for about two or three weeks when the company was again called out & sent to guard the commissary Stores at widow Rouse's. He stayed there until all the corn was fed away to the cattle & hogs when he was sent with the cattle across the southwest fork of New River towards Charleston to a swamp called the Black Swamp where he served the balance of his term in herding the cattle which were then sent off to General Green [sic, Nathanael Greene]. This was about the end of the war. He recollects that he was lying at home wounded when the battle of Guilford Courthouse was fought. He recollects seeing a regular officer on Edenton Road whose name was James Campaign & he thinks was a Captain & did was on his way with some 18 months men to Joined General Greene. General Sumpter [sic, Thomas Sumter] was once in the neighborhood but the did not get to see him. He recollects Col. Craig & Col. George Michell who were Colonels of the militia Regiments & who were with him at the Bridge, also a Col. Hill who commanded a regiment of militia. This declarant has no documentary evidence. Neither does he know of any living person by whose testimony he can procure who can testify to said services. And he hereby relinquishes every claim whatever to a pension or annuity except the present & declares that his name is not on the pension roll of any state. Sworn to & subscribed in open court the 7th day of October AD 1847. S/ George Reed, X his mark

Questions of the Court: 1. Where & in what year were you born? Answer: In King William County, Virginia, on the 12th day of June 1760.

2. Have you any record of your age &, if so, Where is it? Answer: I have none now. The book in which it is recorded is destroyed.

3. Where were you living when called into service? Answer: In Onslow County in the state of North Carolina. After the war, I removed to Charlotte

County, Virginia, & lived there until 1799. I then moved to Kentucky where I lived until about 1815 when I moved to Warrick County, Indiana, where I now live & where I have lived since 1815.

4. How were you called into service; were you drafted, did you volunteer or were you a substitute &, if a substitute, for whom? Answer: Each time I was a volunteer.

5. State the names of some of the regular officers who were with the troops when you served, such continental & militia regiments as you can recollect & the general circumstances of your service. Answer: I recollect General Rutherford (at least I think he was a regular officer) & one Capt. James Campaign who were regular officers. I recollect Col. Hill commanded a regiment at Bluford's Bridge. I first served awhile at Bluford's Bridge & was then sent out onto the Edenton road to protect the Country from pillage about 20 days before this term of service expired I was taken prisoner with John Wilkins, John Loper, John Ferrell, Sandy Rouse & William Bowen. William Bowen was wounded by a bayonet thrust in the neck. I was wounded in the side & in the leg below the knee by a thrust from a bayonet. They, the British, told us we might go home on our honor to go home & for us to go into Wilmington & take

protection. None of us kept this promise except Sandy Rouse. I went home to my father & while my leg was sore from the wound the battle of Guilford Court-house was fought. After I got well, which was a short time after the Battle of Guilford Courthouse, I again served three months in Capt. Ward's company. This time, I stayed all the time at Bluford's Bridge Johnson was Col. & Snead was Major. I again volunteered three months in the Company of Capt. Amos Love the Col. Was John Spicer & the Major was Ephraim Battle, this time I was a short time at Bluford's Bridge when we were dismissed for two or three weeks when we were called out & sent to the Widow Rouse's house to guard the commissary Stores there. I stayed there awhile when the forage gave out, the hogs were sent to John Brinstone's on New River & I went to a swamp called the Black Swamp or War Tom [?] Swamp where I stayed guarding the cattle until my term was Expired, this was about the end of the war. The officers in my first term of service was Col. Thos. Bludworth, Major James Love, & Capt. John McLamma. Each time I volunteered & served as a private soldier in the militia of North Carolina.

6th. Did you ever receive a discharge from the service; &, if so, by whom was it given & what has become of it? Answer: I received a discharge for the last two terms of my service. The first term of my service I was taken prisoner & got no discharge. My discharges were given me by the officers of my Regiment & I have lost them & I believe they were burnt in my house in Virginia which was consumed by fire with everything in it.

7th State the names of persons to whom you are known in your present neighborhood & who can testify as to your character for veracity & their belief of your Services as a Soldier of the Revolution. Answer. Reverend Henry Hart has known me more than 30 years & Colonel John B. Kelly has known me about 27 [? this number is very hard to decipher] years & they I suppose will testify for me.

[Henry Hart, a clergyman, and John B. Kelly gave the standard supporting affidavit.]

Pension application of **Benjamin Taylor** R10406　　f31NC
Transcribed by Will Graves　rev'd 2/18/17

[p 6] State of North Carolina, County of Robeson: Court of Pleas & quarter Sessions November Term 1848　On this 28th day of November in the year of our Lord 1848, personally appeared in open Court, before the Justices of the Court of Pleas and Quarter Sessions now sitting, Benjamin Taylor, a resident of the County of Robeson and State of North Carolina aged ninety-five years, who first being duly sworn according to Law, doth on his oath make the following Declaration in order to obtain the benefit of the provision made by the Act of Congress passed June 7th, 1832. That he entered the service of the United States under the following named officers and served as herein stated: the Field Officers to the best of his recollection were Major __ Russ1 (he thinks John Russ but as to the Christian name he is not certain) but owing to his extreme old age and loss of memory he is entirely unable to recollect the name of his Colonel or Lieutenant Colonel. Thomas Sessions was the Captain of his company when he first was drafted but shortly afterwards he was ordered to Topsail Sound beyond Wilmington where he served for six months under Captain Peter McLama [Peter McLammy], Lieutenant __ Stokesbury (Christian name not recollected) and Sergeant Bloodworth.2 The Captain however was killed by a party of the enemy after he (the said Benjamin Taylor) had been in the service about five months and he remained during the rest of the term under the command of Lieutenant Stokesbury. At the time that Captain was killed he (the Captain) was about 9 miles from the place where Taylor was stationed and sleeping in an old deserted house known as Rouse's House3 without guard or sentinels & the enemy who this affiant was told were Hessians came into the house and surprised and killed the Captain and all his party consisting of thirteen men excepting three who escaped. The three who escaped were Stokesbury, Bloodworth and a private who was wounded and left in the house as dead. The whole number killed was eleven. That he was in no engagement with the enemy during the time he was stationed at Topsail Sound. That owing to his age, loss of memory and the length of time which has

elapsed he is unable to remember the year, or month when he entered the service. It was cold weather when he first went to Topsail Sound he remained through the Summer and came away after cool weather had set in. That he returned home and remained there he thinks about two weeks when Mr. Bloodworth came to his father's house and told him he must return to the Army. That he accordingly went to Wilmington where he rejoined 1 There was a Thomas Russ who served as a Major the Brunswick militia in 1776-1780. 2 This may be an erroneous reference to Colonel Thomas Bludworth. 3 The skirmish at Rouse's Tavern (which this applicant appears to be talking about) occurred in March 1781 at Rouse's Tavern about 8 or 9 miles from Wilmington, NC.

http://www.carolana.com/NC/Revolution/revolution_rouses_tavern.html

the Army under Colonel Young [Henry Young] and the same officers in other respects under whom he had served at Topsail Sound. That he remained at Wilmington six months. At Topsail Sound the whole number of soldiers was about 40, in Wilmington about 60. At the end of six months after he had gone to Wilmington the whole company at that place retired on account of an armed British vessel which came up the River. That he received a discharge from the service given to him by Col. Young – that he kept it for a few years after the end of the war when it became damaged by a storm which blew the water into the house and wet a small bag hanging against the wall in which he kept the discharge with some other papers whereupon supposing that the discharge would be of no use to him he threw it away. He was drafted and lived at that time in Brunswick County and served as a private. He hereby relinquishes every claim whatever to a pension or annuity except the present and declares his name is not on the pension roll of the agency of any State. Sworn to and subscribed the day and year aforesaid.   S/ Benjamin Taylor, X his mark

[p 9: Copy of a marriage bond dated Aug. 18th 1823 issued in Robeson County, NC to John McNatt and Benjamin Taylor conditioned on the marriage of Benjamin Taylor to Lydia Evers in

Robeson County, NC]

[p 17] South Carolina, Marion District   By Samuel J. Bethea Magistrate for said District Personally came before me Robert Taylor of said District who being duly Sworn Saith on oath that he does know and is acquainted with Benjamin Taylor of North Carolina Robeson County and that he does know that the said Benjamin Taylor did serve in the Revolutionary War in two companies six months each at Wilmington Town and at Topsail Sound Sworn to before me this 8 of May 1847.   S/ Robert Taylor, X his mark S/ Saml. J. Bethea, Magat.

[p 15] State of South Carolina, Marion District Appeared before us S. A. Hairgrove and S. J. Bethea Robert Taylor of said District and after being duly qualified upon the Hole Evangelist deposes as follows Interrogatory 1st are you acquainted with Benjamin Taylor of Robeson County North Carolina Ans I am 2. Was he in the American Army during the revolutionary war Ans he was in the Army four years 3th [sic] was he Stationed at Wilmington North Carolina any length of time, Ans he was Stationed there to the best of my recollection six or 12 months 4th was the Stationed at Topsail Sound. Ans-- he was Stationed there a good while 5th what were the names of the officers under whom he Served Ans. Young was Colonel Peter Clanny was Captain I recollect Bloodsworth was an officer but of what grade I do not recollect Sworn to before me this the 13th day of February 1849.   S/ Robert Taylor, X him mark S/ S. A. Hairgrove, Magat S/ Saml. J. Bethea, Magat

[p 22] State of North Carolina Comptroller's Office I, William J. Clark, Comptroller of Public Accounts in and for the State aforesaid, do hereby certify that it appears of record in my office, among the payments made by said State to sundry persons for Military services in the Revolutionary War, as follows, to wit:

Benjamin Taylor Book No. 3, page 20, £9 S2 specie Book A, No. 11 page 71 £13 S13 specie Benjamin Taylor appears as a Corporal in Captain Anthony Sharpe's Company 5th Regiment North Carolina Line, Commanded by Lieutenant Colonel Lytle Muster Roll for the months of March and April 1783, term of enlistment nine (9) months. Return of Col. Wingate, Brunswick County July 9th 1779, Benjamin Taylor In testimony whereof I have hereunto subscribe my name and affixed my seal of office this the 11th of August 1853. S/ Wm J. Clarke, Comptr.

[p 3: Power of attorney dated March 5, 1853, executed in Robeson County, NC, by Lydia Taylor in which she states she is the widow of Benjamin Taylor. She signed with her mark.]

[p 12: Power of attorney dated April 28, 1855, executed in Robeson County, NC, by Isaac Taylor, aged 50, in which he states he is the son of Benjamin and Wilmoth Taylor; that his father died May 10, 1849; that his parents were residents of Brunswick County about 30 years then his father moved to Robeson County about 25 years prior to this death. He signed with his mark.]

[Alexander Humphrey, Daniel Harrell, Daniel McPhail neighbors give affidavits that they have heard it said in the neighborhood that Benjamin Taylor served in the Revolution.]

Pension application of **Ishmael Titus** R10623   f18NC
Transcribed by Will Graves   rev'd 2/14/17

Commonwealth of Massachusetts, County of Berkshire   On this 10th day of October A.D. 1832 personally appeared in open Court, before the Honorable William P. Walker, Judge of the Court of Probate, within and for said County of Berkshire, now sitting, Ishmael Titus, a resident of the town of Williamstown in the County of Berkshire and Commonwealth of Massachusetts, aged 89 years, who being first duly sworn according to law, doth, on his oath, make the following declaration in order to attain the benefit of the act of Congress, passed June 7, 1832. That he entered the service of the United States under the following named officers, and served as herein stated.   That he entered the service of the United States under General Greene [Nathanael Greene] & Colonel Samuel Davies field Officers & Captain John Beverly Company Officer. He cannot state nor does he recollect the day, month or year he entered the service.   He entered the service on the Atkin [sic, Yadkin] River in the County of Roan [sic, Rowan] & State of North Carolina.   He was in an engagement at Guilford [Guilford Court House March 15, 1781] under Colonel Samuel Isaacs and Captain John Beverly in this engagement Colonel Isaacs was taken and carried to Augustine by the British, in one other engagement at Deep River under Colonel Absalom Cleveland [sic, Benjamin Cleveland], in one other engagement at Kings Mountain [October 7, 1780] under Colonel Cleveland. He fought at Guilford, Kings Mountain, at Deep River as stated above. He marched through the State of North Carolina.   He was a substitute for Lawrence Ross who was drafted. He was born a slave in the County then called Amelia below Lunenburg in the State of Virginia to Harry Bluford, lived with him till he was about 13 years old and was then sold to John Muir & Dick Muir [possibly John Marr and Richard Marr??] who lived on Dan River in the State of North Carolina. He lived with them a long while does not recollect how long & was then sold to Lawrence Ross with whom he lived at the time he was a substitute for said Ross. For his being a substitute for Lawrence Ross who was his master he was to have his freedom. He cannot state when he left the service on account of his ignorance being brought up as a slave – he was in the service three years as a substitute to Lawrence Ross who was drafted for that time. He served under Col. Absalom Cleveland & in the Company commanded by Captain John Beverly he knew General Morgan [Daniel Morgan], General Gates [Horatio Gates], General Greene [Nathanael Greene], Colonel Absalom Cleveland & Captain John Beverly. He has no documentary evidence of his services & knows of no person whose testimony he can procure to testify to his services. He never received a discharge from the service. He has no record of his age. He lived when he was a substitute for said Ross & at the time he entered the service with said Ross on the Atkin [sic, Yadkin] River in the County of Rowan & State of North Carolina and after he was discharged he lived at [illegible name, looks like "Minich"]1 near New Rochelle from there he moved to Ballston in the State of New York from there he went to Troy in said State of New York from there to Bennington in the State of Vermont & from there he removed to Williamstown in the County of Berkshire & Commonwealth of Massachusetts, where he now resides & has for the last 15 years. He is acquainted with Rev. Ralph McGridley, Thomas F. Coxsey, & Stephen Hartford, Chiny Taft who reside in said Williamstown will testify as to his character for veracity & their belief of his services as a soldier of the Revolution. He hereby relinquishes every claim whatever to a pension or annuity, except the present, and declares that his name is not on the pension roll of the agency of any State.   S/ Ishmael Titus, X his mark Sworn to and subscribed the day and year aforesaid. S/ W. P. Walker, J. Probate

I, Ishmael Titus, of Williamstown in the County of Berkshire and Commonwealth of Massachusetts being duly sworn according to law do on my oath make the following additional declaration in order to obtain the benefit of the act of Congress passed June 7th, 1832. That I cannot by reason of old age and the consequent loss of memory swear when the battles mentioned in my former declaration took place, but I find from the History of the Revolution that the Battle of Kings Mountain was fought in October 1780 and that

Colonel Cleveland commanded at that time as mentioned in my former declaration. I also find from History that the Battle at Guilford was fought in March 1781 which I was at as mentioned in my former declaration. I was also at Gates' Defeat [Battle of Camden, August 15-16, 1780] did not arrive there till the American Army began to retreat. This battle I find from the History was fought in August 1780. I was one of the number who retreated to Salisbury. I entered the service in the spring of the year more than a year previous to Gates' Defeat which must have been in the year 1779. The statement in my former declaration that I was in service three years as a substitute for Lawrence Ross who was my Master, is wrong. I was a substitute for said Ross for one year only and this year was previous to any Battles during this time some skirmishes took place among the Tories & Indians was stationed during the winter at a place called then Fort Independence. After the year was expired for which I was to have my freedom as stated in my former declaration I enlisted into the Army during the war during the term of my enlistment the Battles mentioned were fought. I was discharged on the Holston River at a Log Court House, he cannot recollect the name of the place this was at the close of the war. I served not less than the periods mentioned below and in the following grades. For one year as a substitute for Lawrence Ross, I served as a soldier. For more than two years I served (having enlisted) as a soldier and for such service I claim a pension. When I entered the Service as a Substitute, I entered in Captain James Davis' Company Colonel Samuel Isaac' Regiment under General Greene. When I enlisted I enlisted under Captain John Beverly in Colonel Cleveland's Regiment. I enlisted at Salisbury. I recollect that when I entered the service it was said that war had existed about four years.   S/ Ishmael Titus, X his mark

I, the above named Ishmael Titus, being duly sworn do on my oath make the following affidavit in addition to my former declarations, viz.: When I enlisted, I enlisted under Captain John Cleveland, son of Colonel Absalom Cleveland. I stated in my former declaration that it was in Captain John Beverly's Company. I recollect now that he was the man to whom I made application to be enlisted & not the

Captain of the Company. One other fact which I omitted to state before, I now recollect, viz.: After I was dismissed at Holston River after the war was closed, coming home to Yadkin River, I (with ten others) was taken upon the top of the Allegheny Mountains by a party of Tories headed by a man they called Captain Bill Riddle. I recollect it was on Thursday in the afternoon we were carried back to the foot of the Mountain & there kept all night with our hands tied & a guard put over us the next day a guard was over us all day, our Muskets being taken from us. On Saturday they brought to us Col. Cleveland as a prisoner & bound him in the same manner. The next morning, I was sent by the Tories to look for the Tories' horses. I found all but one & took them back to the Tories. Then I was sent to search for the other horse on horseback, while looking after this horse, I discovered two companies under the command of Captains Cleveland, they inquired if I knew anything about their Father Colonel Absalom Cleveland. I told him where he was & went with them to the place where the Tories had him. Colonel Cleveland as soon as he saw them said ["]Come on my Boys,["] when they rushed forward & shot at the Tories, they wounded one in the back, the rest fled into the Woods we then all of us came home. Some one or two months after this, I saw all but one of the Tories viz. (nine) hung at Rowan Court house. Dated at Williamstown, this fifth day of December A.D. 1833. S/ Ishmael Titus, X his mark

State of North Carolina Secretary of State's Office I William Hill Secretary of State in and for the State aforesaid do certify, that the name of Ishmael Titus does not appear on the musterrolls of the Continental line of this State in the revolutionary war, or any other document affording evidence of service in said line. There was a Colonel Cleveland (a Militia Colonel) who I believe was at the Battle of Kings Mountain and I believe there was an Officer of the name of Isaacs, but I have no recollection of a Captain Beverly, or to have heard of such an Officer. John and Richard Marr lived on the waters of Dan River, and owned or were interested in the Iron works called "Troublesome Iron works" – Given under my hand this 2nd October 1833 S/ Wm Hill

Made in the USA
Lexington, KY
22 August 2017